Wreck Me FOREVER

POLISHED P&P
SERIES

CHAPTER ONE
LUCAS

Groaning, I brushed my free hand through my shoulder-length blond curls and then tapped my phone against my forehead. Why did my brother have to have his biker friends over tonight?

Yes, it was his house.

Yes, he could do what he wanted in it.

To some extent.

I could have gone without seeing him drilling one of his flings over the kitchen table. A table where I would always make sure to sit at the opposite end after witnessing that scene.

It was just that I'd had a shit day. One of the worst.

I'd woken late because I'd forgotten to set the alarm. It had rained, which caused me to get drenched, and then I'd slipped as I walked into class, landing on my ass. I was sure it would be bruised by tomorrow. Of course, everyone had a good chuckle over it. Lastly, I nearly got run over on the way home. The stupid dick didn't want to give way to a pedestrian and decided my life was fair game.

It was lucky I moved out of the way fast enough. Though, as I did, I got a good look at the driver. Mitch dickface Henry. He and I had gone to the same high school, and I'd hoped to be rid of him through college, but I wasn't. He had it out for me, always had, ever since it was proven that I excelled in class. He wanted to be the best, but there I was tarnishing his perfect grades with my better ones. It wasn't like I meant it. I just loved learning.

I could still hear his taunting laugh.

When would the dweeb grow up?

With a shake of my head, I finished my walk down the street to my brother's place. It was two months ago when our parents moved from Nevada to Australia, and sold their place, to see if it suited them in retirement. So, Zion, my brother, offered up his spare room so I could stay and finish the fourth year of my pre-med degree, then med school before I found a placement and started my residency training at a hospital.

I'd been surprised he'd offered it to me. Zion was five years older than me, and we were so different from each other, it was funny. I was the nerd, the quiet guy who was clumsy, spoke before he thought—or stumbled over his words—and was uncomfortable in crowded rooms. Zion was the life of the party. Popular and fun-loving, he didn't care what anyone thought. Unfortunately, I did, but I was slowly learning not to.

What helped when Zion offered his place was that we both knew we would be busy and hardly be in each other's space since I liked a place where I could study in peace. Which I did a lot. When I wasn't in class, I had my head buried in a book. I had a job at the local café, which also contained an electronics store where I helped out with repairs on gaming systems. Zion was busy with the business he'd gone into with some of his friends.

Our parents were proud of him, especially since Polished Pussy was doing so well. Even if it was a brothel, our parents didn't care as long as Zion was happy in what he was doing. Mom had wanted a tour of the place, but when Zion said it was open day and night and that he wouldn't feel comfortable taking her through a place where people had sex, she'd glared and asked, "How do you think you and your brother were made?"

I quickly ran from the room before I heard any more, but Mom got her tour and had come home gloating about how she knew it would expand because of how clean it was and how sweet the ladies were. No doubt she would have sat down and found out about the working girls' lives while sipping tea and probably commenting on their skills.

I shuddered at the thought. However, Mom was right. Zion and his friends were opening another two Polished Pussies in the neighboring cities in the next month.

Heck, I was even proud of my brother. I never thought a brothel with the name Polished Pussy would take off.

I'd been wrong.

When I'd asked him about the name, he'd snorted and said, "We'd been throwing names around all night, but then, after a few joints, someone said they'd like to polish their woman's pussy with their tongue. We all looked at each other and yelled, 'Polished Pussy.' It stuck, and thank fuck it worked."

I wish I hadn't asked. I didn't need to know about his friend wanting to… do *that* to a woman.

You see, my brother didn't know I wouldn't want to talk about women and their body parts. He didn't know that it didn't interest me, because he didn't know I was gay.

Our parents didn't even know.

Why I hadn't told anyone, I didn't have a clue. I knew they would support me, but every time I went to open my mouth to inform them I liked dick, I felt it wasn't the right moment. Instead, time passed, and I kept my mouth shut. In the end, they moved without the knowledge, and I shifted into my brother's home. My brother, who was the straightest guy I knew. I wasn't even sure about his stance on gay people, which was another reason I hadn't said anything.

I couldn't exactly say, "Ah, hey, bro, what do you think about guys getting it on?" No matter how I said it, I knew it would come out wrong, then I would freak out if I thought he was going to be disgusted.

Now, I had to go into his house full of his friends, who I hadn't met before, and pray I didn't check any of them out too long. Sighing, I closed my eyes and rested my head against the front door. Already I could hear the voices of Zion and his friends. They had music playing in the background, but what it was, I didn't have a clue.

Straightening, I brushed my hands down my NASA tee and then reached out to the handle. Before I could grab hold, the door got swept open, and I stumbled forward so hard my head collided with a crotch. As I landed on my hands and knees, my head slipped down further and rested against someone's muscled thighs.

The only problem with Zion's house was the open-floor living.

Laughter filled the area.

"Brothers, I'd like you to meet my younger, and clumsy, brother, Lucas."

A hand under my arm helped me. Actually, it practically lifted me on its own to my feet. "You okay, kid?" the large man asked.

"Yes," I squeaked. I cleared my throat and punched my chest, then lowered my voice. "Ah, yeah, I'm good."

The man smiled. His perfect white teeth between his trimmed beard captured my attention. He seemed in his mid-forties, but he looked good for it. His salt-and-pepper hair was styled back in a ponytail. He nodded. "Good. Sorry about the abrupt open. Thought you were some crazy fucker staking out the joint or the pizza guy."

I nodded. And kept nodding since I didn't know what to say.

"Name's Death." He held his tattooed hand out that was attached to his tattooed arm. I noticed his other arm was also inked.

Nervously, I licked my lips and stared at the large appendage—meaning his hand—that was still outstretched toward me. His name sounded like he would use his hands to kill people. I was too young and small, well, compared to him, and nice to die. Still, even when my hand shook, I pushed it forward and gripped his. "Lucas," I said.

Death snorted. "Already heard."

I wanted to slap my forehead. "Yeah, right." I forced a laugh.

Using my hand, he pulled me further into the room, then he dropped his hold and pointed to another huge guy. "That's Quake, Torch, and the prospect. He doesn't get a club name until he's a full member." I nodded to them all. Quake was a solid man, heck, all of them were, but he was the biggest. His hair was blond and messy, and it went perfectly with his sea-blue eyes. Torch had a buzz cut and a cold look in his eyes where I worried if I looked too long, I would ask for forgiveness even when I hadn't done anything. The prospect was the youngest. Where I was twenty-two, he seemed to be in his early twenties also, but it was hard to determine just what his age actually was.

The front door opened abruptly behind me. I bit my bottom lip to keep in the scream. But that didn't stop me from jumping and stumbling as I turned, and if it wasn't for Death's hand wrapping around my arm, I would have met the floor once more that night.

However, when I looked up, I realized there was still a possibility of dropping to the floor. The most gorgeous man I had ever seen stood just inside the doorway, scanning the room. If it wasn't for his hands fisted at his sides and the scowl on his face, I may have fallen to the floor in awe of his beauty.

I took another quick glance around the room and noticed my brother did, in fact, have some good-looking friends. All of them could be on the cover of a magazine. I wasn't sure what it was about the scowling man that set me off in a sweating, peeing-my-pants, "holy crap he's looking at me" moment with my pulse racing, but he did. His dark brown hair was shaved at the sides, and the top was longish and messy, some of it flopped in his dark green eyes. He would probably punch me if I tried to push his hair back though. He was tall, my short frame only reaching his shoulders. His tight black tee showed off the muscles in his arms, and his dark ripped jeans surrounded thick thighs.

I jolted and pulled my gaze up quickly when Death said, "Wreck, you took forever, fucker. Get in here and meet Saint's brother, Lucas."

Saint?

Who was Saint?

I wasn't a brother of Saint.

"Lucas, I'm Saint. It's my club name," Zion called; he must have seen the confused look on my face.

Nodding, I glanced back to Wreck and did a lame wave before I grabbed my own arm with my other hand. "Ah, s'up."

S'up?

Was I a gangster now?

"I mean, hi."

He lifted his chin, and out of his mouth came a gravelly, "Hey." He looked at Death. "Pizza guy just pulled up." Then he walked by us and aimed for the kitchen.

I wanted to follow like a stray kitten. He could take me in, pat me, love me…. Dear God, I'd finally lost it over a good-looking *straight* guy.

A slap to my back had me clamping my lips together and eyes widening. "Fuckin' pizza, gotta love that shit," Death said before he moved toward the still-open front door.

I heard a greeting before my arm was snagged, and Zion dragged me from the room, down the hall toward my bedroom. Had I done something already?

In my room, Zion closed the door and turned to me. "Are you okay with this? We've been on a long road trip and were close by, so instead of heading back to the compound, we stopped here for some food and drinks."

I waved a hand around. "It's fine." I laughed. "Totally fine. I mean, it's your place. You can do whatever."

His eyes narrowed as he crossed his arms over his chest. "Are you okay?"

"Yep," I popped and nodded. I threw an arm out. "I mean, I know you've been with your group—"

"Club. The Diamond MC," Zion stated with a smirk.

"Right, the MC club for a while. I just thought that if I ever met your guys—"

"Brothers." He chuckled.

"Yep, um, brothers, that they'd find me, ah, not cool."

Zion snorted. "Is this you being worried about what they'll think of you because you're gay?"

My heart stopped, my breath caught, and I wheezed, "You know?"

Zion smiled. "Shit, Lucas. Mom, Dad, and I know. We've known for years now."

I felt sick to the stomach. "How?"

"Besides the fact you look at guys before women?" he asked. I glared and nodded. He grinned. "Mom found some gay porn on your laptop one day when she went to use it."

I didn't have to see to know I'd paled. I *felt* the color drain from my face.

I sat on my bed with my head in my hands. "That's just so wrong on so many levels." I looked up. "I won't be able to face her. I'll have to leave the family."

Zion laughed, and I wanted to punch him. Heck, I'd never been a violent guy, but I was suddenly seeing the appeal of smashing someone's face in.

"Relax, I'm messing with you. It was me who found the porn, but I'd already suspected. Mom just asked me one day if you'd said anything to me about liking guys."

I dropped back on the bed and covered my face. "Obviously I'm terrible at hiding it."

"Bro, we're family. We're gonna notice more than anyone. None of my high school friends suspected. What I don't get, though, is why you haven't told us?"

I groaned. "Is now really the time to have this talk when you have friends out there?"

"Yeah, it is." He moved over to my bed and sat next to me. When I didn't move, he shoved my leg. "Seriously, bro. Why didn't you say anything?"

I shrugged. "I don't know. I just got used to keeping it quiet."

"You know we don't care, right? You're you, no matter who you want between your sheets."

"Zion," I groaned, heat hitting my face.

"It's true."

Sighing, I finally sat back up. "I kind of knew you, Mom, and Dad would be okay with it. But even though it seems more accepted this day and age, Zion, it doesn't make it easier to come out. There's still haters."

"Some people just need to be taught a lesson. If anyone fucks with you, Lucas, you tell me."

Rolling my eyes, I gave him a small smile. "I can take care of myself. When I'm ready, I'll tell whoever I want I'm gay, but I want to be comfortable within myself first. I've only... had one, um, you know, experience...." I rubbed the back of my neck. "But I haven't... there hasn't been anyone special in my life to date."

"I get it. Just as long as you know I have your back. Mom and Dad will as well. But also, my brothers won't be like any of those bigoted fuckers," he stated. "Hell, if they are, they'll deal with me."

I bumped his shoulder again. "You're an okay kind of brother, Zion."

He snorted. "Just okay? I'm the best. Now, you gonna come out there and have some pizza?"

"Give me a minute, and I will."

His hand slapped down on my shoulder and squeezed. "You got it." I watched him walk from my room, and in a way, it felt like a small weight had been lifted off my shoulders. I should have guessed my family would have known I was gay even before telling them. They did know me the best. Even if Zion traveled in different circles to me, he'd always made sure he was there for me if needed. I just never asked.

I'd promised myself when I moved out of the family home and into Zion's that I would start living and being who I really wanted to be.

I guessed it was time to begin.

Glancing to the closed door, I heard deep laughter down the hall. There were *bikers* out there. Bikers I didn't know. However, they did seem like okay guys, and I knew my brother wouldn't be a part of their group… club if they weren't, but could they honestly accept me?

I wasn't sure, and that was damn scary.

Still, it was worth a try. It was probably time I did come out of my shell. I hadn't had many friends in high school. Those I had had gone off to different colleges. Those who stuck around made new friends, and we'd drifted apart. Though, I was lucky enough to have a couple of friends from college where we got together every now and then to catch up and wind down from studies.

So, it could be good to go out there and make new friends.

Another roar of laughter filled the house.

Then again, friends were overrated.

*B*y the time I pulled up my big guy boxers and made it out to the living room, I came to an abrupt halt. There on the couch sat my new porn star, and he was playing... *playing* my vintage Nintendo.

"Hey, Lucas, I saved you some pizza. It's in the fridge," Death called from the kitchen where he stood with Zion, Quake, and Torch.

"Ah, thanks." I smiled; it may have been wobbly from my nerves, but I meant it. Though Death was my brother's friend—they all were—they'd been nice to me so far.

This night felt so draining, and it wasn't even eight yet.

"You need to jump higher. Higher," the prospect guy said loudly as he shifted to the edge of his seat. Wreck grunted but otherwise ignored him. "Go up. You gotta go up. Jump, Wreck, jump."

"Double-tap to jump higher," I suggested. Wreck did, and he went higher on the jump, getting the star Mario needed to collect.

"This yours?" Wreck asked in his deep, rough voice.

"Yep?" I said hesitantly, which made it sound like a question, nervous from having his attention on me.

He looked at me and then back to the screen.

I moved closer. They both seemed engrossed in the game, which was good to see. Mario would always be a favorite played by many, but the old Mario game was still the best. I glanced over my shoulder into the kitchen area. Zion already looked my way; he gave me a chin lift with a smile. I knew what he was saying, even without the words. *"Go on, get in there, and play. You know you want to."*

I did because, well, it was Mario. I hadn't expected a biker would want to play. Wreck's large hands seemed awkward as he tried to press the buttons on the small controller. Admittedly, I feared for my controller.

My nerves twisted my insides as I shifted closer again and sat on the couch armrest. I bounced my leg up and down, so I didn't reach out and grab the controller from Wreck's hands.

Wreck.

What type of biker name was that? How did he get it? From wrecking people's lives? From wrecking women's bodies?

I nibbled on my bottom lip and pushed all thoughts of Wreck in the bedroom from my mind.

Yes, he was more than good-looking. He was throw-my-money-at-him and bow-before-the-stunning-god, but I refused to allow myself and my lust to get in the way. He was straight, well, I was fairly sure he was since I'd never seen a gay man who could scowl so much. So, he was beyond my orbit, and it would do me no good to keep thinking of him in more ways than eye candy. My emotions liked to glue themselves to unattainable men, and since the last one crushed me into the dirt, I wouldn't let my emotions control me.

Elliot had been one of my friends at high school. We'd been close, and I'd been in love with him for a year, but as soon as I hinted toward liking guys, he'd screwed his face up, told me to fuck off, and that he never wanted to see me again.

Huh, maybe that was another reason why I didn't like people knowing I was gay.

"Wanna play?" came a growly bedroom voice. Damn, I had to stop that. He didn't have a bedroom voice.

I glanced at Wreck to see he held the controller out to me.

The prospect harrumphed, "It *was* my turn, or we could just do two-player like I suggested."

Wreck ignored him and stared at me. His gaze penetrated me in ways I wished wasn't the only thing penetrating me. Something only one other had done, and that was two years ago, and the experience had been horrible. Still, it was one I wanted to try again with the right person. I blushed and shook my head, "Ah, it's, um, okay, he can have a go."

Wreck's brows dipped. He said nothing else and dropped the controller onto the prospect's lap.

I had to get away. It would be best for my sake to stay far away from the man who'd captured my attention. Far away.

I got up and walked into the kitchen. Death greeted me with a smile as he handed me a beer. "Here, kid, suck this down."

We heard a snort from the living room and then "Think he'd rather suck something else down."

I stilled as my face burned more than it was. I focused on Zion; his face had darkened. He looked thunderous with his upper lip raised and aimed in the living room.

"Fuck," Death muttered, his eyes over my head.

We all heard a cry of pain. I spun back to see Wreck had picked up the prospect, thrown him across the room, and was stalking after him. The men around me raced into the living room where all I could do was stand still and witness the power behind Wreck. All while trying not to pee myself.

"The fuck you say?" Wreck demanded low.

The prospect scuttled back on his hands. "Sorry. I'm sorry. I didn't mean it. It wasn't supposed to come out. Fuck, *fuck*, sorry." He glanced at me. "I'm sorry. Shit, I didn't mean to say it."

Before I could answer, Wreck had a grip on the prospect's tee and pulled him to stand. He shook him. "You disrespectful motherfucker. In Saint's home, you say that about *his* blood brother. *His* family."

"Wreck," Zion called.

Wreck shook the prospect again. "Who the fuck you think you are?"

"No one. I shouldn't have said anything." His eyes slid to me again. "Sorry, I…. Fuck, it just popped out since I thought he was good-lookin'. I was gonna ask him out."

With that bomb dropped, the room fell silent. My heart beat frantically behind my ribs. He'd thought *I* was good-looking and was going to ask *me* out. Not that I would have said yes. He wasn't my type, unlike the man holding him, but it was nice to know I wasn't repulsive.

Heck, I was still in shock by his admission, even if it was fake or not, and it seemed I wasn't the only one. They all stood around, staring at the prospect like he'd grown a dick on his forehead.

Though, they could be thinking he was an idiot for telling everyone what he'd just said or for even thinking it. Maybe he was the first gay or bi biker they'd come across and were trying to understand what language he was speaking.

"Well shit," Death said, then chuckled. "Wreck, put the dickhead down."

Wreck didn't. It seemed like he wasn't listening to anyone, and I didn't want anyone's death on my conscience, so I moved closer. "Hey, ah, Wreck… it's… he's— You can put him down. I know I say some things without thinking all the time, and, um, he says he didn't mean to say it aloud."

"I didn't. I swear."

Wreck dropped the prospect to the floor. He turned to me, glared, and then walked right to the front door. As soon as he was out, he slammed it closed after himself.

A hand slapped to my back. Zion pulled me aside while the others warned, and then teased, the prospect. "Don't worry about Wreck. He's a little protective of people in the club since we're his only family."

"But… I'm not in the club."

Zion smiled. "You're my kid brother, you're family. Plus, he also doesn't like fuckheads. The prospect has been gettin' on his nerves all day, and that was the final straw, obviously."

All I could think of to say was "I'm not a kid."

Zion chuckled and went back into the kitchen, where his other friends had drifted off to. I jolted when I heard next to me, "Yeah, sorry again about that." The prospect stood beside me, a slight pink to his cheeks. "Do you think they give a fuck I just outed myself?"

My eyes widened. "You… they, ah, you're gay?"

He chuckled and rubbed the back of his neck. "Bi, actually. Was worried about how'd the brothers would act, but they seemed protective of you."

This was all too much for my little but smart mind to handle.

I scrubbed a hand over my face. "Yeah, I don't think you'll have to worry about them." At least I hoped not. I didn't know how many were involved with the club, but if they were anything like the men in the house, then he shouldn't need to worry. I really had to find out more about my brother's friends.

He smiled. "Name's Kylo, and I wasn't playin' you when I said I was gonna ask you out, but I know it's a shit time now after everything. So, friends?"

Taken back again, my eyes widened as I looked down at his outstretched hand. Slowly, I took it and shook. I nodded. "Friends." Because going on a date with him was the last thing on my mind when it hadn't finished processing what had happened since I walked into the house.

"Cool. Wanna play?" He tilted his head toward the Nintendo.

"Sure," I replied hesitantly because this whole experience seemed as if I'd been kidnapped and placed on a different planet where everyone was accepting and amazing and scary and hot.

Once I sat on the couch, Kylo passed me a controller and got onto the area where we had to pick another player. "Heard Zion say you were at college. What do you study?"

"Medicine. I'd like to become a doctor. A pediatric doctor, in fact. Um, what do you do?" I asked as I picked Luigi to help Mario through the worlds.

"I work in a gym owned by the club." He shrugged. "I like it. I get to use the equipment whenever I want."

Zion had said the club owned many businesses, but he was just one of the club members who had put money in with the brothels. I took a quick glance at Kylo's body. Only when I lifted my eyes, he was already looking at me and smiling.

He winked. "What do you think, has it paid off?"

My face ignited. "Ah, yeah?"

He chuckled and bumped my shoulder with his.

"So, ah, the way Wreck was with you... were you worried?" Because I couldn't help but think that if I'd been Kylo, I would have crapped my pants. Yet, even though his voice had been high in worry, other than that, he didn't seem too concerned. Unless those types of situations happened all the time. I didn't know how bikers acted or what their lives were like. Maybe I should have watched *Sons of Anarchy* when it was first out, then I could have some insight into what to expect.

Kylo snorted. "You haven't been around brothers before?"

I shook my head. "No. I've been busy. I knew Zion was in a club, but until tonight, I'd never met anyone before."

"Strange, your brother's been in the club for ages."

"Four years, but again, I've been busy. School has ruled my life for a long time. It still does because I know what I want in life, and I want to achieve it." I shrugged, suddenly feeling bad because I should have known more about my brother than what I did.

"Don't stress. I can understand that. You're focus-driven. It's cool. To answer your question though, you gotta understand the brothers in the club are... shit, how to explain?" He went quiet for a moment. "It's like these men protect in their own kinda way. They have their own laws, and they stick to them. They'd do anything for anyone in the family, no matter the cost, because they believe the brotherhood, their families, are everything. They live and breathe

the club. It's their life. I've never had structure in my life. My parents are fucked-up drug dealers. An old friend of my father's got me out of it and brought me into the fold by takin' me in. I've been around their ways, and it suits me perfectly. It's why I wanted to patch in and become a member."

I nodded, not really knowing what to say.

He went on. "They deal in respect and don't like being fucked around. It surprised me the way Wreck was, but I understood I went too far. They don't like shit bein' said. Wreck was only teachin' me a lesson. Yeah, he might have been rough, but it's their way, and by doing it how he did, I know I'll never make the same mistake again."

"But, ah, wasn't it a shock he did it over you saying something that was, well, small?"

He chuckled. "Yeah, it was a shock, but I disrespected you in front of your own brother and in his home. It wasn't right."

I still wasn't sure I completely understood. I didn't think I ever would, but who was I to judge them and their ways? I couldn't and wouldn't. If Kylo wasn't upset over the incident, then I couldn't be. Also, a warm feeling in the pit of my stomach emerged, knowing I'd been protected by a stranger over something so insignificant.

I felt Kylo's eyes on me and heard his chuckle. "It's okay. You'll get used to it."

Again, I wasn't sure I would. However, now living with Zion, I guessed I would maybe bump into more of his friends—*brothers*—if they dropped by, so in time, I could understand what it was all about being in a club as such.

Or maybe I would stick to asking Zion about it since he was my brother, and it would be better if I wasn't around his good-looking friends and making a fool of myself.

My attention went back to the game, and as we traveled through the worlds, we chatted about everyday things. It was different, already it felt easy, like I'd known Kylo for a while. I glanced over my shoulder when I heard footsteps and found Quake and Death coming our way.

"Prospect, my turn now," Death said.

I stood, holding out my controller. "It's okay, you can have this one. I've got to go make a call anyway."

I caught Zion looking at me from the kitchen. I wasn't running off if that was what he was thinking.

"You sure?" Death asked.

"Yep. I need to call our parents, and it should be morning there in Australia."

He tipped his chin up and took the remote with a smile. "Cool."

I started for my bedroom. "Yo, Lucas," Zion called. "Tell 'em I said hey."

"No problem. I'll also tell Mom about the women constantly showing up for a piece of—"

He actually paled as he barked, "You'd better not say shit."

Laughing, I told him, "Don't fret. I've got your back."

He studied me for a moment before smiling. "Yeah, and I got yours."

I went back into my room and pulled my phone out of my pocket. It was funny how a shitty day could turn into an all right night—a night where things could change. And if it wasn't for my brother's faith and trust, I wouldn't be calling our parents right then to tell them something they already knew but hadn't heard from me.

It rang a couple of times before my dad answered with "G'day, cobber. Struth, it's a hot one."

Closing my eyes, I ran a hand over my face. "Dad, have you actually heard anyone talk like that since moving to Australia?"

He chuckled. "Well, no, but if I keep doing it, I'll bring the trend back in."

"I highly doubt it. Now, is Mom awake?"

"She's awake and—"

"Is that one of my boys?" I heard yelled. "Gerry, is it one of my babies?"

"She's coming this way," he finished.

There was a scuffle, and then through the phone came, "Hello? Lucas? Zion?"

"It's Lucas, Mom."

"Oh, my dear boy, how are you? I miss you and your brother so much. I never should have moved so far away. Gerry, we're moving home. I want to go home."

"Lucy, you promised me another six months. We're staying another six months."

"Fine," she snapped. "Lucas, tell me everything that's going on. How's living with Zion?"

"It's good, Mom. I actually need to talk to you both. Can you put me on speaker?"

"What is it? Are you hurt? Is Zion okay? Did you steal drugs off some pimp, and now they want to sell your body?"

"Jesus Christ, Lucy, where did that come from?"

"I write books for a living, Gerry. My mind tends to overreact."

"Overreact my ass. You're just crazy."

Sighing, I sat down on my bed and waited until they stopped yelling at each other. If I didn't know they loved one another, I would worry about their marriage.

Things calmed down after Dad said, "You're an amazing author, honey. I just worry about your sanity."

"So do I."

When I heard lips smacking together, I yelled into the phone, "Mom? Dad?"

"Sorry, dear, what were you saying?"

Shaking my head, I told her. "You don't have to fear, Mom, I didn't steal anything, no one wants to sell me, and Zion is well."

"That's great to hear. Then what did you have to tell us?"

"I'm gay," I announced before they started running off with any other thoughts.

"What did I need to say?" was whispered by Dad. "Got it." He cleared his throat. "What, boy? You're gay?" he yelled. I rolled my eyes and let it play out. "I can't believe this. It's such a surprise. I don't think my heart can take it. Oh look, your mom has fainted from the shock. I think… and I'm sorry to say this… but I need to disown you."

"Are you done?" I asked in a flat tone. Mom's giggle sounded through the phone.

"I think so," Dad answered. "Am I done, Lucy?"

"Yes." I could tell she was smiling from the lightness in her voice. "Honey, we've known you were gay for a long time. Why it took you so long to tell us, I'll never know. But now you have, and no matter what, you should know you have our love."

Warmth spread through my chest. I closed my eyes and bit my bottom lip because it threatened to tremble.

"But," Dad added, "like we've told Zion, the same rules apply to you. Even if it's a guy you're bringing home to meet us, make sure they're not drug dealers or takers, ex-cons, or pimps. Wait, lawyers. We don't need any lawyers in our family. Your mom dictates enough around here."

There was a slap, and then Mom cried, "Hey."

Laughter burst out of me. I'd been so scared because of all the bullshit I'd seen and heard about other people. I should have trusted my family.

"Love you, guys," I told them.

"Aw, we love you too," Mom cooed.

Dad grunted. "Yeah, what she said."

"Say it, Gerry."

"Lucy."

"Say you goddamn love him also."

"Fucking hell. I goddamn love you too, kid."

By the time I hung up the phone with them, I was still laughing. More weight had lifted from having such an amazing family.

CHAPTER THREE
LUCAS

I had my head buried in my books at the kitchen table when I heard, even over my music, the front door open. Of course, I was at the other end of the table from where I saw Zion going at it, while trying to put that moment far from my mind. Thankfully books distracted me when I got in the zone. I flicked to the next page and lifted my foot onto the chair while leaning onto my opposite arm on the table as I absently called, "Hey," when I felt my brother move closer.

He said something, but I was too busy writing down another note to answer or actually take in what was said. So I replied with "Uh-huh," then nodded and jotted down another note before sticking the pen back in my mouth and turning the page in the textbook again.

The music I had softly playing from the speaker in front of me on the table suddenly stopped. Scowling, I lifted my head. The pen dropped from my mouth, and my heart gave a lurch behind my ribs.

Wreck stood beside the table with his arms crossed over his chest. His glare sent shivers down my back.

"A-Ah, hi," I offered before I thought about hiding under the table to get away from his stare. Instead, I braved it to add, "Zion should be home soon." I shrugged.

"I know."

Okay.

Was it suddenly hot in the room? Perspiration beaded between my shoulder blades, and at any moment, my tee and sweatpants would become embarrassingly damp. If Wreck wasn't there, I would be fanning myself, but his intense gaze drilled into me.

I wish something else would drill— Do not go there, Lucas.

"You're not listenin' again," Wreck growled sharply, causing me to jump.

"Sorry?"

His jaw clenched, like he ground his teeth together. "This area isn't the fuckin' safest. You had the front door unlocked, were listening to goddamn music, while your head was buried into a book oblivious to the world around you." He leaned down and planted his hands on the table. "I could have killed you at least twenty times before you even noticed I was in the damn house."

I scoffed. When his eyes darkened more, I quickly pretended it was a cough and then said, "I knew someone was in the house. I called out."

"You didn't even look up." He straightened and threw out a hand toward the front door right when Zion opened it and stepped in.

He paused and looked from Wreck to me and back to his friend. "What's goin' on?"

"Your brother is an idiot," Wreck stated.

"Am not," I yelled, and regretted it since it sounded childish.

Zion snorted. "What did he do?" He moved into the living room, then passed us and went directly to the kitchen to get two beers out of the fridge.

"He had the door unlocked while having his head in a book and music playin'. He didn't even look at me when I entered. Didn't even listen when I said I was goin' to kill him."

Had he said that?

Well, dang.

Zion passed the other beer to Wreck and rolled his eyes. "He's always like that when he's studyin'. I'm sure the house could burn down around him, and he wouldn't even notice."

Wreck's brows dipped lower, and he was back to glaring at me.

"Whatever," I said bravely. I wouldn't let Wreck's fierce look intimidate me, not when I found his concern over my well-being sweet. I picked my pen back up and looked down at the textbook again. Zion grabbed Wreck's attention when he started talking about his motorcycle, and I went back to reading.

At least I tried to, but I was sure my body was on fire since I could feel Wreck's gaze burning into me every now and then.

It had been a couple of weeks since I saw him last, which was when we'd first met. Two weeks went by, and I hadn't even thought of him. Okay, a total lie, but I kept it to a minimum of two thoughts a day. Now he was in the house again, and all I wanted to do was listen to his gruff voice and stare at him so he could star in another fantasy.

I'd lost count of the times I'd masturbated while thinking of Wreck, of how he had me pinned to the wall instead of Kylo. But the difference was, I'd been wrapped around Wreck in a lover's embrace.

A laugh escaped me. If he knew what he did to me, he would freak out. Why, oh why, did I have to find him the most attractive out of Zion's friends?

Kylo had kept in contact, and we were becoming closer. Why couldn't I be attracted to him? Heck, even Gregory, a guy in one of my classes, had approached me just yesterday and asked if I wanted to get coffee. He was nice, sweet, and cute, yet I said no instinctively. I'd said no because my stupid head wouldn't stop thinking of the muscular Wreck.

I didn't even know his real name for crying out loud.

I guessed no one listened to me from the heavens when I'd

prayed that I didn't want to see the man again so I could get over my attraction.

My phone chimed with a text, and I smiled. It was Kylo. I opened it; he was asking me if I wanted company. I nibbled on my bottom lip as I thought about it. He'd popped by a couple of days ago, and we'd listened to music while eating Chinese takeout and talking. It'd been good. We'd laughed and got along really well. I could see him becoming a good friend.

However, I did have to get at least three more chapters done before I went to bed. Even though it was Friday, I liked to get as much done as I could before I had work the next day.

"Who's that?" came barked next to me as a plate was deposited on the table next to my arm.

I glanced up. Wreck stood there, staring down at me. Did he ever not glare?

"Um, a friend."

"Eat" was all he said before stepping back into the kitchen where Zion was.

I glanced down at the plate and found two grilled cheese sand-wiches. My stomach growled loud enough both my brother and Wreck looked over.

"See, he forgets to eat when he's studyin' too," Zion supplied. Wreck's gaze narrowed once again as he grunted. It had me wondering if he grunted like that when he came.

Sighing, I pushed that thought away and picked up a sandwich. I put my music back on, since it wasn't so loud they wouldn't be able to talk to one another, and as I ate, I forced my mind back into my work.

It wasn't until I'd written my last note that I dropped my pen and stretched. Opening my eyes, I saw Zion, Wreck, *and* Death looking at me from where they sat at the end of the table.

"When did you get here?" I asked, reaching out to stop my music.

Death and Zion chuckled, while Wreck's lips twitched, but he didn't indulge in the hilarity the others had found.

"What?"

"Kid, you are somethin' else," Death said.

"What?" I asked again.

"I got here about twenty minutes ago, came in, said hi, you ignored me, and since then been shootin' the shit and watchin' you totally in your own fuckin' world. No wonder Wreck was worried you'd get killed. Lock the damn door when you're home alone."

"I second that," Zion said. "Bro, I didn't realize how bad you were until now. When you get into your head, nothin' will pull you out until you're done."

Rolling my eyes, I stood and picked up my plate. "I'm not that bad."

"Kid, we could have had a ragin' party, and you wouldn't have heard shit."

"That's unlikely."

"Bro, seriously, you're like in your own bubble and nothin' will get through. You need to make sure you still know what's goin' on around you. Are you like that when you go to the library?"

"No, I'm more aware." I moved off into the kitchen and knew they were all looking at me.

"I'm callin' bullshit," Death said.

"Dammit, Lucas. It's fine to do it here, as long as you lock the doors—"

"And windows," Wreck added.

Zion nodded. "And windows, but don't do it anywhere else. People could steal off you, and you wouldn't even know it's happenin'."

"They could slip him something, and he wouldn't know," Wreck added.

Dropping my plate into the sink, I spun back around, tripped, and stumbled forward before righting myself and snapping, "I'm twenty-two years old."

"He's twenty-two?" Death asked.

"Twenty-two?" Wreck mimicked, eyes narrowing. "I was sure eighteen at least."

"He's always looked young," Zion said.

I growled in the back of my throat in annoyance, and they all smiled at me, even Wreck. Like I was some cute little puppy. "I'm twenty-two and I *can* take care of myself. Nothing has happened—"

"Yet," Wreck put in.

I scowled at him. "Nothing has or will happen. I'm not a kid who needs coddling, so effing quit it."

"Effing?" Death asked, smirking.

"He means fuckin'," Zion said and then shrugged. "He doesn't like to swear." They chuckled.

I threw my hands up in the air and stalked by them to the hall-way. I would hide in my room until they were gone. It was Friday night after all, and I was sure they'd be off partying soon. Only then I remembered I hadn't replied to Kylo, so I turned back around and thumped my feet back out to the table where— My phone wasn't there.

"Where's my phone?"

"Who's Kylo?" Wreck asked. He had my phone in his hand on the table.

"Isn't he the prospect?" Death asked.

Zion laughed. "Which one?"

Death drummed his fingers on the table in thought and then said, "Yeah, he was the one that was here that night. Hey, are you two a thing now?"

Oh my God. They were here to drive me insane. Screw my fantasies about Wreck or how good-looking Death was. I was going to kill them. As soon as I found a way to do it where I didn't have other bikers hunting me down when they found out.

"It's none of anyone's business. Pass me my phone." I leaned over the table with my hand held out.

"No, seriously, are you two datin' or somethin'? He shouldn't be goin' after my brother," Zion said with a snarl.

"We're not dating," I yelled, straightening with my hands on my hips.

Everyone went quiet and stared at me, as if waiting for an explanation.

"Did he reject you?" Zion asked darkly. "I'll kill the little fucker for rejectin' you."

"I'll help," Death added.

This was one effed-up situation, and my head spun from it.

Before Wreck could join in on the threats, I said, "No, he didn't reject me." Zion went to open his mouth, but I shot my hand out and up. "Stop. Don't say anything else." I took a breath. "Kylo and I are just friends. Again, not that it's anyone's business. And even if we were dating..." I blushed. "Um..." I forgot what I was saying because I really couldn't believe I was talking to three men about my nonexistent dating life with a guy. "Look, let's, ah, leave it at it's no one's business."

They all looked at one another, making my body tense up. "What was that?" I demanded, pointing at all of them.

"What?" Zion asked casually, leaning back in his seat.

"That look," I stated.

"There was no look," Wreck said with a smile, and that smile made me stupid because it was stunning.

"I... you...." I growled again before reaching over, snatching up my phone, and stalking from the room while three men laughed behind me.

In my room, I closed my door and went straight to my bed and lay down. The scene rolled around in my head, and I still couldn't make sense of it. Yes, it was normal, well somewhat, for my own brother to be protective of me, but then there were Wreck and Death doing the same.

Unless... unless it was the way they were. Like Kylo said, they took care of their family.

Groaning, I dropped my arm over my eyes. I couldn't help but hope that Wreck was doing it for another reason, but thinking that made me even stupider.

I just had to remember and keep it in the forefront of my mind that these men would do anything for their family, and since I was Zion's brother, it looked like it meant me as well.

A gasp escaped me when my phone chimed on the bed beside me. I removed my arm and picked up the phone; it was Kylo.

Kylo: Hey, I know you're probably studying, but have a break. Instead of me coming over, if you're free, live a little and come to the compound.

Me: I'm so sorry for not replying earlier. You're right, I was studying. Maybe next time I'll take you up on that offer, but right now, I'm tired. Plus, I have work tomorrow.

Kylo: You'll always have work on Saturday. What about tomorrow night?

Me: Sorry, I promised an old friend we'd go to the movies.

I wasn't lying either. West and I were friends since the first day of college. Usually Kimber, Janine, and Linton would be with us as well, since we all met on the first day and became somewhat friends, but they were all busy. Not that it bothered me. I was a little closer to West than the others. Mainly because we'd been drunk one night and confessed we were gay. There was zero attraction between us though; we never saw each other as a fit.

I sat up as a thought crossed my mind. What happened if Kylo thought I was being rude and not inviting him along? Would he want to go? Did he have time? He'd told me he usually manned the bar on the weekends at the compound, which, when I asked, I found out was the place the bikers got together for their meetings and such. Some even lived there.

Would West mind if I asked Kylo?

Me: Would you want to join us?

Kylo: Thanks for the offer, but another time. I've got shit to do at the compound.

Me: No problem. Talk tomorrow.

When he didn't reply straight away, I knew he must have been caught up doing something. I went back to lying down on the bed. Sleep called to me, and since I was done with the books, I needed to have a shower before I could even think about shutting down.

Moaning, I got up and grabbed my towel that hung over the back of my desk chair. I wouldn't leave it in the bathroom since the last time I had, a woman had come out of the bathroom with it around her naked body. It was weird knowing I dried my balls on the towel that sat snugly against her skin.

Opening my door, I made my way into the bathroom. Before I could close the door, my brother called.

I stuck my head out and asked, "Yes?"

"We're headin' off to the compound, wanna come?"

"Thanks, Kylo has already asked, but I've got work tomorrow, and I'm tired from studying. I'm going to shower and head to bed."

"Kylo asked?" Zion questioned.

Was I going to get Kylo in trouble if I said yes? But it was too late since I'd already said he had.

"The prospect asked him?" came from the living room in Wreck's rough tone.

"That's what he said," Zion called. He glanced back to me. "Right?"

Stepping out of the bathroom, I crossed my arms over my chest and said, "If I say yes, you can't say anything to him."

Death's head peeked around the corner. "Sure, kid, we won't say anythin'."

I narrowed my eyes. "Your smile says different, Death." I glanced back to my brother. "Kylo is allowed to ask people to the compound, right?"

Zion nodded. "Yeah, he can invite someone."

"Then it's okay he asked me?"

Zion shrugged. "Sure."

"What am I missing here?"

Death snorted. "Prospects are only allowed to ask someone they're into. Usually it's women."

My face heated. "He's not into me. We're friends."

Zion rolled his eyes while Death laughed and moved off to the front door.

"Let's go," Wreck called.

"Wait," I said to Zion. I moved down the hall. "How come you can ask me, and I'm just your brother, but if Kylo does—"

His hand shot up. "You're family. It's different for family. Kylo wants a piece of you."

"He doesn't!" I shouted.

Zion smirked. "Fuck, you're blind. Don't worry, bro, he'll get the point that you only want friendship."

"Maybe I shouldn't have accepted his offer for dinner Sunday," I muttered more to myself.

Zion chuckled, slapped my shoulder, and walked away.

I was sure Kylo and I had been on the same page—just friendship.

"Yo." I looked up to see Wreck at the front door, my brother and Death not in sight. "I'm lockin' the fuckin' door on the way out."

I wasn't an idiot. I would have locked it before I crashed. I didn't reply. All I did was nod. Wreck glared at me a little while longer before stalking out and shutting the door. Then I heard the handle jiggle as he made sure the lock was in place.

I couldn't stop the smile claiming my lips before I quickly wiped it away when I remembered Wreck was straight, at least I was fairly sure he was, and just looking out for Zion's brother… who he probably thought was an idiot.

CHAPTER FOUR
LUCAS

West was laughing so hard he had to hold his stomach. I let him have his moment because if it happened to anyone but me, I probably would have found it funny as well. We'd been to the movies already and were sitting at a late-night café to grab a coffee.

He slapped the table. "Only you could be surrounded by bikers and have one confess he wants to date you."

I glared. "That's not true. You know my dating life is nonexistent because no one has shown interest."

He scoffed. "Please. What about that guy from class? He saw me with you and looked like he wanted to strangle me to get to you."

Rolling my eyes, I shook my head. "He asked me for coffee, but I couldn't go."

"Couldn't or wouldn't?"

"Couldn't." Wouldn't because a certain man had been on my mind. "But I think I'll take him up on his offer now." I had been stupid not to accept the chance to get to know him. He was cute and sweet like I'd thought, and I was wasting my time thinking about a man who was completely different from me.

"Good, you two could hit it off. He was cute."

I nodded. "Enough about me though. How's things been for you?"

He waved a hand around. "Same old. Your life is completely more entertaining than my boring one."

"I doubt that. What happened with that Sam guy?"

West actually blushed. I used to think he was one of the biggest flirts out there, but he was just always touchy and nice to everyone. He'd met Sam about a month ago when we'd been out for drinks one night. We all could see the sparks flying.

"He's great." He smiled shyly.

"Oh my God, you love him."

"What? No, it's too soon for that." His gaze traveled off, and he was back to smiling sweetly.

"You make me sick with how in love you are," I teased.

His eyes snapped to me, and he reached across the table to shove me. "Stop it."

"Lucas" was clipped.

West and I both stopped, and slowly, we dragged our eyes to the side of the booth and up, up some more, until they paused on Wreck standing there glaring down at us.

"W-Wreck, um, what, ah, what are you doing here?"

"Wreck, baby, you promised me some cake." A red-haired woman stepped up beside Wreck and curled herself into his side. "Hi," she said to West and me with a smile.

Sliding my hands under the table and fisting them as a pang of sadness swept through me, I quickly fought that feeling, pushed it right back down because it was stupid to have for a now obviously straight man. *I should have gone with my gut feeling about Wreck being straight.*

Instead, I smiled and said, "Hi, I'm Lucas. Zion's—I mean Saint's brother."

"Aw, that's the sweetest. I'm Hailey." She looked up at Wreck with a smitten smile and said, "No wonder you wanted to come over." He glared down at her, but she didn't seem fazed, implying it was his usual expression.

Clearing my throat, I said, "And this is West, a friend of mine."

"Hi, would you both like to join us?" West offered and then grunted when I kicked him under the table.

"Yes," Wreck stated. He shoved Hailey to West's side. I quickly had to move over or else the brute of a man would have sat half on me. Even though I'd squished myself in the corner, I could still feel his body heat.

"But, baby, I thought we were grabbing cake to go to, you know…" She giggled. "Eat it off each other."

"Isn't that sweet," I said sarcastically since I was on the verge of gagging. Hailey giggled again, and I wanted to rip out her vocal cords.

Whoa, I had to back the heck off, and, from a kick to my shin, West saw it as well. I glanced at West, but his eyes were on the man beside me, and they were wide. I chanced a look out the corner of my eyes and shifted my eyes back to West when I noticed Wreck glaring down at me.

"Wreck, baby, can we get out of here? Leave these two on their date?"

"It's not a date," West said.

Just as I blurted, "That might be good."

Dang it all to hell.

West and I stared at each other.

"We're good to go," Wreck said, and then he was out of the booth and stalking to the counter.

"It was nice to meet you both." Hailey grinned, and she was quickly following Wreck with a sway to her small hips. Nearly every man watched as she went by. I didn't see the appeal. Yes, she had curves and boobs, but… who was I kidding? She was stunning. No wonder Wreck had her on his arm. Was she his girlfriend or just a hookup?

"I don't think you can glare someone to death," West offered.

"What? I wasn't."

West's brows damn near met with his hairline. "Can I ask what that was all about?"

"That was Wreck. A friend of my brother's. From the biker club."

"I got that from the patch on his biker vest. But what I was asking is what's up with you and him?"

I jerked my head back in confusion. "What do you mean? Nothing."

"Uh-huh."

Shaking my head, I told him, "You're being weird. How can you get from that there's something going on? There's nothing going on." He stared me down. "Okay, so I may have a small crush on him, but that's about it."

"All right, that explains why you wanted to kill Hailey. But it doesn't tell me why he stared at you as if… as if…."

"As if he wanted to choke me?" I shrugged. "I annoy him. He thinks I'm an idiot, that's about all."

"Uh-huh."

"I really hate it when you say that."

He smirked. "I know. Still, I don't think it was a look of annoyance."

"Whatever it was you thought you saw, I don't want to hear it. I'm pushing Wreck from my mind and getting over this infatuation I have with him. In fact, the next time I see Gregory, I *will* be asking him for a coffee."

West smiled at me. "Good luck with that."

"Thanks," I said, but from his chuckle, I had a feeling he meant something else.

My mind was still on Wreck and his actions as I waited for Kylo the next night. I couldn't help but think about why Wreck even approached my table in the first place.

My phone chimed; it was Kylo saying he was on his way. I

quickly sent back a thumbs-up and was happy he hadn't canceled altogether. I'd been worried my brother and his friends would say something to Kylo, but it was obvious they hadn't since he was still meeting up with me.

All I had to do was make sure Kylo understood why it wouldn't be good for us to see each other… that was if the others were serious about Kylo inviting me because he liked me or if it was them just messing with me. Which wouldn't surprise me.

I heard Kylo even before I saw him. Glancing out the window, I saw him pull up on his bike. He slid off and removed his helmet. He caught my gaze and waved, and I returned it.

The bell above the door sounded as he entered.

"Hey," he said, putting his helmet on the booth seat opposite me before he sat next to it.

"Hi, glad you made it safely on that thing."

He laughed. "You can't seriously say you don't like bikes. Your brother has one."

"Oh, I know. I tell him how unsafe they are, but he just laughs at me and shakes his head. I guess it'll be something I just won't understand the appeal of."

"Have you ever been on one?"

"No, and it'll never happen."

"We'll see."

"It won't."

He just smiled, so I shook my head. I knew I wouldn't get on the back of a bike. I always thought it would look silly for a guy riding on the back of another guy's bike anyway. More people could assume two guys on a bike meant they're gay and cause problems. Also, I really was terrified of them. There was nothing around you to protect your body if an accident occurred. Give me a car surrounded by metal, and I was fine.

I jumped when a voice beside us said, "Hi, I'm Mabel, and I'll be your waitress tonight. Can I get you guys a drink?"

Kylo laughed at my reaction but managed to get out, "A coffee, please."

"I'll have the same," I said.

"Great, I'll grab those while you two have a look at the menu." She quickly moved off, well, as fast as an eighty something-year-old could.

"She owns the place with her husband, who's a good ten years younger than her. They're into swingin' and often have a third partner in bed," Kylo announced.

I lifted my wide gaze. "How do you know?"

"I don't. But it was funny to see your face."

Glaring, I kicked across under the table and connected with his leg. Of course, he was still laughing.

After we ordered, I heard another rumble of engines pulling into the parking lot.

"Fuck," Kylo clipped. "I told 'em I wasn't comin'." He ran a hand over his face. "Now they're gonna give me shit."

"Why?" I whispered. "And why would you tell them you weren't coming?" I added quickly.

He sighed. "They were givin' me hell about invitin' you to the compound."

"I told them not to say anything to you!"

He snorted. "Like they'd listen." He shook his head, and we both glanced over to the door when a grinning Death, a smirking Zion, and a scowling Wreck entered.

Kylo glanced back to me and quickly said, "I'd told them when I invited you, that we were just friends. Of course they didn't believe shit because of that stupid rule for prospects. But seriously, Lucas, I know we're just friends, and I lied to them about coming because I'm a fuckin' idiot."

Well, at least in all that, I knew Kylo was on board with where we stood with one another.

"Prospect, didn't think you were showin'," Zion said. He stopped beside the booth while Death went up to the counter, saying something to our waitress. Wreck stood beside Zion and shoved at Kylo's shoulder.

Kylo moved over for Wreck to sit and said, "I shouldn't have lied, but I was always comin' to see Lucas. Since we're friends."

Death appeared and snorted. "Friends."

Kylo threw up his hands. "What does it matter? You guys won't believe me anyway."

"Shift over, bro," Zion said. I did, and he slipped in beside me while Death pulled a chair over to sit on the end.

"We're just givin' you shit." Death laughed. "We believed you after you took that pretty blonde woman to bed last night."

"Then what are you all doing here?" I asked, refusing to look at the man next to Kylo. He looked too good in his jeans, long-sleeved black thermal and his biker's vest.

"We were in the neighborhood," Zion replied, with a smile that told me he was lying—even though our place was just down the street.

I rubbed a hand over my face, suddenly tired. I didn't understand why they concerned themselves in Kylo's and my affairs, but they were. Unless it had something to do with Kylo being a prospect to their club. Were they worried about his actions and how it would look toward the club? But then they weren't anything but playful about it all.

It all had to come down to Zion being my brother. He could still be concerned Kylo was messing with me in some way. Maybe he didn't believe we did only see each other as friends. I supposed it could look different since Kylo asked me to the compound, and we were meeting here for dinner. However, it didn't mean they had a right to be in our business.

"Is this because you're worried about me or because Kylo is a prospect to the club, and you're concerned about his actions?" I just had to ask and search for answers, or it was going to drive me insane.

Death shook his head. "The prospect knows not to fuck you over, or he'd have all of us after him."

I groaned. "We're friends."

"Yeah, we're seein' that, but with Dad and Mom away, it's up to me to take care of you," Zion explained.

My blood boiled. Slowly, I faced my brother. "Unless I ask for help, I would prefer if you stayed out of my business since I am twenty-two freaking years old. I can take care of myself." I ground my teeth together and took a breath. "I appreciate your concern, but for the love of God, don't worry about me."

"Freaking." Death chuckled. Wreck smirked, and even Kylo laughed, until I shot him a glare.

Zion simply grinned. "Got it. You can deal with guys on your own until they fuck with you then, and I fuckin' mean this, Lucas, then you come to me, and I'll deal with them."

Closing my eyes, I dropped my head back and groaned. Straightening, I nodded. "Fine."

"Dinner," Mabel announced with her hands full of plates. She set mine down, then Kylo's, but she also had a plate of pizza.

Zion grabbed a slice right when Mabel said, "I'll be right back with the rest."

"Ah, aren't you all leaving now?" I asked.

Zion winked. "Bro, since you and the prospect are just friends, it means we're stayin' for dinner too."

Damn it all.

"We're dating," I blurted, hoping to get rid of them.

They all stared at me and then laughed. So now they wanted to believe me? I glanced at Kylo, who was smiling. He shrugged.

I could start talking about anal penetration and was sure that would have them running from the place in seconds screaming. However, I wasn't sure I could pull it off without blushing or stumbling over my words. There was even a chance I'd yell something I shouldn't. So, since there wasn't anything I could do to get them to leave, I started eating my hamburger.

"Hey, Lucas, where you work, do you fix phones as well as gamin' systems?" Death asked.

"We have someone for phones since I'm mainly for the gaming consoles. But if you want, I can take a look. I know a few things."

Zion laughed. "A few things. He knows about everythin'."

Rolling my eyes, I said, "I'm not that good."

"See, Wreck, knew Lucas would be able to fix your phone."

Wait… it was for Wreck's phone? Was it too late to take back everything I said? What happened if I looked at it and saw things I shouldn't?

A hand with a phone came into view. I looked down at it like it was going to bite me. I glanced up and met Wreck's eyes.

"Here," he clipped.

I quickly took it and placed it on the table. "I'll, um, ah, take a look as soon as I've, ah, finished eating."

I caught Zion looking at me like I'd grown another head, or he was possibly just thinking about something.

"No problem," Wreck said just as Mabel showed with another two plates.

The rest talked as they ate, all while I stared down at the phone next to my plate. You could tell a lot about a person and what they had on their phone. What would Wreck's tell me? I wasn't sure I wanted to find out, not after meeting his girlfriend, Hailey.

CHAPTER FIVE
LUCAS

*A*fter taking a quick look at Wreck's phone, I realized it was going to take me longer than I thought.

Glancing up at him, I asked, "So it won't move from the Apple logo?"

He shook his head. "Been like that all day."

"Right, well, you want to hope it'll only need an upgrade but if it's a system reboot, you're going to lose everything on there. Still, for both I'm going to need my laptop, which is at home. Can I take it tonight?"

He grunted. He was a man of small noises or words unless I annoyed him. Boy, did I hear about it then.

"Do you have things backed up and saved to your cloud?"

"Nope."

Damn. I dropped a nervous laugh. "You won't kill me if I can't get everything back, right?"

His stare suddenly felt intensified. But it didn't tell me if it was a yes or a no.

I gulped. "Right?"

The others at the table chuckled. Zion patted my shoulder.

"Relax, bro. We'd figured as much. Wreck said he doesn't keep anythin' important on there anyway."

It probably just held all his hookup numbers or naked photos of women. In a way, I kind of hoped it would need a system reboot. It meant all his numbers would disappear. I snorted to myself over the thought that Wreck could easily add more. I was sure he wouldn't be at a loss for women wanting to offer them up.

"What's so funny?" Wreck asked, his voice startling me.

"Nothing."

He eyed me like a bug under the microscope.

I shrugged. "I was just thinking of something."

He wouldn't look away, and sweat started forming on my brow.

"I, um… I was thinking of, ah, that…."

"Wreck, leave the kid alone." Death smiled, and I could have hugged him for butting in. Especially since he also drew Wreck's attention away from me and onto a subject about business. I quickly put Wreck's phone in my pocket and picked up my drink. That was when I caught Kylo looking at me. He raised his brows, glanced at Wreck, and then back to me with a smirk.

"What?" I mouthed.

He shook his head, but he did it smirking still. What was he thinking? Why did he look at Wreck and then me? What did he see that no one else saw? Did he think I had a thing for Wreck? I didn't. I mean, yes, Wreck was good-looking. Okay, he was better than that, but there wasn't a rule against me admiring his features. Did I stare at Wreck too long? It was all about his looks. Damn Wreck and double damn Kylo. This was confusing me and sending me spiraling with too many thoughts.

Kylo chuckled, obviously seeing my panic setting in.

I scratched my chin with my middle finger, which only made him laugh louder. Of course, it brought all eyes to us.

"What's so funny?" Death asked.

"Nothing? I don't know. Kylo's being weird." I blurted each out, one after the other, and now they were all staring at me. I glanced down at the table and saw the menu. A menu I wanted to pick up so I could use it as a fan because the room had heated. I cleared my throat, lifted my gaze, and announced, "I think I'll get home now, since, ah, I have to work on Wreck's phone, and I still have a bit of studying to do."

Suddenly my phone rang. Thanking God for the interruption, I answered it quickly without looking at the caller ID, "Hello?"

"Did you ask him out?" came West's voice, but it was loud, too loud.

Blushing, I pulled it away, fumbled it around, near dropping it, all while West continued, "Come on. You said you were going to ask him out. I've given you a day—"

"West," I shouted, just as I switched it off speaker. I held the phone to my ear and ducked my head. "Now isn't a good time."

"Lucas, you can't tell me Gregory didn't give you his number. I thought you would have done it before you chickened out."

"West," I whispered harshly. "Now *really* isn't a good time. I'll call you as soon as I get home."

He groaned. "Fine, but if you don't call me by nine, I'm calling back."

"All right," I snapped, and then hung up the call. I shoved at Zion, who was laughing. I could also hear a couple of other chuckles. Thankfully, my brother moved, and I slid out of the booth. At the side, I pulled out some money, threw it on the table, and then mumbled, "Bye. Wreck, I'll give Zion your phone once I'm done. He'll get it to you." With that, I quickly walked out of the café.

On the way home, all I could think about was burning myself in the backyard. I never wanted to see any of them again. It was fine for them to know I was gay. Heck, I was completely fine with it since Zion gave me the confidence to be myself around them. Kylo also helped since he didn't hide who he was. However, for my private life to be shoved in their face was embarrassing. They didn't need to or want to know about my dating life. I also didn't want them to know since it was hard enough when they thought Kylo was into me.

It was safer I kept my private life behind closed doors. Safer for them so I wouldn't kill them if they said or did something I didn't like. Safer for whomever I chose to date, and safer for me, so I didn't die of mortification.

I kicked at the rocks on the walk home, finding for once I wanted to curse. I could swear at myself for being such an idiot for having it on speakerphone in the first place. Somehow, I must have run my finger over it when I answered. Not only was I stupid for that, but for agreeing to help Wreck with his phone. I should have said it would be better for Benny at work to fix it. Then again, I hadn't known it was for Wreck when Death asked.

"Idiot, idiot, idiot," I ranted as I hit my palm against my forehead. Sighing, I stomped up the stairs and unlocked the front door.

All right, I just had to push it all back and distract myself with something. The best thing would be studying, and while I did that, I would plug Wreck's phone in to see if I could fix it.

It was an hour later when I remembered to check if Wreck's phone had finished charging. When I'd first checked it, I found all it needed was an upgrade. I also did a virus protection scan and found a couple I had to delete. I'd been surprised when I bypassed it that his phone didn't have a passcode to get into it. Wreck didn't lock his phone at all. Although, it was Death or Zion who said he didn't have anything of importance on there. It made me wonder what he did have on there. However, I'd put it aside until it finished charging. Now it was staring at me, just asking to be checked out, much like his ass did.

Would it be bad to snoop?

Could he find out?

If he found out, would he kill me?

I kept reaching for it only to stop short and pull my hand back. I ran a hand over my face and groaned. It was such a temptation.

My phone sprang to life, and I yelped at the sudden sound. My heart raced in my chest. Grabbing it, I looked at the ID, and when I answered, said, "West, I nearly peed myself. Maybe text before you call to warn a guy."

He laughed. "What were you doing that was so distracting to get scared in the first place?"

"Nothing," I said.

"That was too quick. You were up to something. Tell me."

"I was studying."

"Sure you were. Wait, were you jerking off? I can go if you need to finish."

"Heck, West, that's… just no, and I wasn't."

"All right," he drew out, sounding like he didn't believe me. "Anyway, where were you that you couldn't tell me if you asked Gregory out?"

The memory had me cringing. I tried to deflect the subject instead with "Just because you're happily in love doesn't mean I'm going to jump on board right away."

He snorted. "Please, I knew if I didn't hound you, you would chicken out."

I huffed. "I won't chicken out. I'll ask him tomorrow when I see him."

"Great, I want to hear all about it."

"Fine."

"Good."

"Awesome," I snarked. "Now, I better get back to work before I need to sleep."

"Wait one second, you still didn't answer me on where you were when I called."

Damn it all.

Heck, why not just tell him? So I did, and then I hung up on him laughing.

Only then, I went back to staring at the phone on my desk.

A small look would be okay.

Slowly, I reached out and picked up the object. It felt heavier for some reason. Maybe it was the guilt I was projecting into the phone that made it heavy.

Did it stop me though?

No.

A nervous flutter filled my stomach when the screen lit up. Earlier, I'd noticed he didn't have a background picture, just the standard factory setting. I went into photos in case he didn't have any to pick from. I was wrong.

There were over fifty photos of women posing in some way. All flirty, all sexy, all sickly. God, he really did have a slew of women. It said Hailey wasn't his only one, else she would have gone hissing mad about it all.

Did he have a different one each day of the week?

How was that possible?

He was older than me, and even I wanted a release three times a week. Okay, it was nearly every day if I was honest. But that was only because, since meeting Wreck and his damn good-looking face and body, my fantasies were all twisted up and had me ready to explode.

Feeling sick, where even my stomach twisted in an uncomfortable way, I got out of the photos. I had a chance to look at his text messages. With Zion not home, I was all alone, but I felt that was going too far. I also didn't want to throw up by the messages I would see with his women.

Instead, I opened his browser to the web. He'd been looking up local builders. Boring.

However, when I went to his history, I froze.

No way.

No effing way.

Oh my God.

I dropped the phone and stood. I gripped my hair, and my eyes were so wide I was sure my eyebrows were making out with my hairline.

"Holy shit," I whispered. The moment called for a swear word. It really did.

I sat down, only to get back up and to pace. "I don't understand... why?"

My hands shook. I flicked them out and around. My heart was kissing my chest, it beat that hard and fast, while my stomach dipped up and down like it was on its own roller-coaster ride.

I wished I didn't have that information. I didn't know what to do with it. What was I supposed to do with this?

It wasn't good.

It wasn't good at all.

If I could kick myself in the ass, I would have right then. I should have left the phone alone. I shouldn't have touched it.

Now I had.

I had, and my emotions had burst to life.

Grabbing the chair, I collapsed back into it and picked up the phone again. My hands trembled as I slowly brought the screen closer, and then I pressed the button to show what I'd seen.

It was still there.

Plain as day and I couldn't believe it.

Why?

I rubbed at my eyes in case I was seeing things. Opening them, it still showed the same.

Why?

Dear God, why had Wreck been looking at porn?

Porn!

It wasn't only that, but it was *gay* porn.

Right there on the screen were two men doing it.

Two *men* making love.

It was hot, it was slow, and it was nothing I expected to see in his browsing history. I glanced at the date of it. It'd been just the other day.

Wait… maybe it was a trick. I laughed to myself half-heartedly, even when I wanted to throw up. Would they be that hard up for a laugh and give me a phone with gay porn on it to test me to see if I looked at it?

But now I had, I couldn't unsee it.

How would I act now?

Was it real?

Did Wreck look at this video? Was it someone else on his phone? Could it be Zion, Wreck, and Death playing a trick on me?

Shaking my head, I had to think they wouldn't stoop so low. Would they?

I groaned; it almost sounded pained. I didn't want to second-guess their actions, but there could be a small chance.

I couldn't ask Kylo as there wasn't a chance I would breathe a word about this to anyone.

Heck, I wouldn't even act like I'd peeked into his phone.

Nodding to myself, I realized that all I had to do was never see Wreck again. I would give his phone to Zion, and I wouldn't have to face him. He didn't need to know I was aware he'd looked at gay porn. I pinched the bridge of my nose in frustration. That was if it was Wreck looking at it in the first place.

I would keep my mouth shut, and no one would know anything.

If I did come face-to-face with Wreck, then I would act normal. That, or I would run and hide.

Actually, running and hiding sounded good.

Someone knocked on my door. I screamed and then yelled, "One second."

"Bro, if you're whackin' off, I'll talk to you in the mornin'."

"Oh my God," I yelled while getting out of Wreck's history and then the internet. "Why does everyone think I'm masturbating?"

Zion laughed. I stomped to the door and opened it sharply. "Here," I snapped. "I fixed Wreck's phone. Give it to him tomorrow."

"Will do." He grinned.

"What did you want anyway?"

"Just to say I was back, saw your light on."

"Right." I nodded. "Okay." I gave him a thumbs-up.

"Are you okay?"

"Great. Perfect. Peachy."

Zion snorted. "Are you sure you weren't whackin' off?"

I stepped back and slammed my door in his face. He just laughed it off, and then I heard him shift down the hall to his room.

CHAPTER SIX
LUCAS

*I*t had been a week since I worked on Wreck's phone, and I still couldn't get it off my mind. It plagued me in my sleep, schooling, and study. I was a mess, and it was all my own fault. I was a fool for being nosy and looking at his phone, so I had no one else to blame but me.

Sighing, I dropped the textbook on my desk. I leaned back in the chair and rubbed a hand over my face. I was tired, but I wanted to read another chapter before I stopped and watched some Netflix to wind down. I was supposed to be out with West and the rest of the group, but I canceled since I knew West would annoy me for not having asked Gregory out as yet. I wasn't in the right frame of mind to do it. It wouldn't be fair to Gregory. My eyes drifted down to the note that fell out of my bag. I opened it again and read over it.

I'M GOING TO FUCKING KILL YOU.

Rolling my eyes, I knew who it would be from. Mitch. There wasn't anyone else who hated me so much. After seeing the note, I refused to take it seriously, and he was stupid if he thought I would. What in the heck was his problem? If it was only because I bested him in classes, it was ridiculous. For now, I would ignore it. I didn't have the energy to worry about Mitch being ridiculous. I had too much on my mind.

Thankfully, I hadn't seen Wreck since last week. Even when he was around here the other night, I managed to hide in my room until they'd left. And the time I'd seen him down the street, I'd quickly turned around and walked the other way. All while trying not to poop myself in nerves.

If he questioned me, I was scared I would cave and tell him I looked at his phone, found some porn on there, and would probably ask if he knew he was looking at the wrong site. He needed the one with boobs and dicks, not all cocks.

"Forget it," I said to myself. I shut the book, turned, and went to my door. Since Zion was about to leave, I would take over the living room and eat my share in popcorn drizzled in Nutella. I opened my door, yelped, and stumbled back. When my legs hit my bed, I dropped down and sat.

"Zion's out there somewhere," I told the one man I didn't want to see while I pointed behind him.

"Saw him pullin' away when I arrived," Wreck explained, well, his version of an explanation; it didn't tell me what he was doing there.

I nodded. "Okay," I drew out. Why didn't he follow after Zion?

"You saw it," he growled.

My heart had only started to settle from the fright, but once more, it rattled like crazy around in my chest. "W-What? I-I don't know?" I laughed nervously. "Saw that you're, ah… standing in my door and scaring me? Then yes."

Wreck stepped in and closed the door behind him.

Was this the time he would kill me?

"W-What're you doing?" I glanced everywhere but at him. I couldn't look at him because there was a high chance I would pee myself.

He stepped closer. "You've been dodgin' me, why?"

I quickly stood and shifted to the side, so there was more room between us. I shrugged and moved over to my desk and faced away from him, where I reached out and straightened some books. "I, ah… don't know what you're talking about." I fixed the pens I had lying around. "Did you, um, need something?"

My pulse sped, and my body locked when I felt heat at my back. I swallowed thickly when his rough voice caressed my ear. "You drive me fuckin' insane."

How? Why? The questions were stuck in my throat.

"So goddamn insane." His voice was lower, gruffer.

Please tell me why, I pleaded silently.

He didn't tell me though.

He didn't say anything else.

But then he showed me what he meant.

Suddenly, I was gripped and spun around. Large hands held me, one at the back of my head and the other at my waist. It all happened so fast I didn't register where they were until after lips pressed down onto mine.

Time stopped.

The room stilled.

The kiss didn't go further. He just pressed his lips against mine as if he was frozen. I went to push him back, and maybe he sensed my intention because his fingers threaded into my hair, and the grip had me gasping. That was when he slipped in his tongue to touch mine. It didn't stop at one touch. He used it to claim my mouth in a heavy, demanding, and so very hot kiss.

"Yo, Wreck? Lucas?" was called. Next, Wreck shoved me back. I hit my desk, and my things scattered everywhere. He took a step away with a panicked look on his face while he wiped at his mouth.

That hurt. It cut into my chest.

Although, since I knew Zion was coming down the hall and we couldn't be caught in a situation Wreck obviously didn't want to be seen in, I ordered, "Give me your phone and sit in the chair."

Surprisingly, Wreck did, and just as the door opened, I was

already pointing at something on Wreck's phone. "That's how you use it. If it happens again, you might be better seeing Benny at the shop."

"Got it," he bit out low.

"Good. Hey, Zion, I thought you'd left?"

"Yeah, I did, but I forgot my wallet. What's goin' on? Why you here, Wreck?" he asked, looking at both of us.

Since Wreck wasn't going to say anything, I did. "I just fixed Wreck's phone again," I said as Wreck stood and faced Zion.

Zion's eyes narrowed. "Okay. Why was the door shut?"

I snorted. "I didn't even realize it was. Anyway, I've got shows to watch, popcorn to eat, and since I'm done with Wreck's phone, he can go with you."

Zion's suspicion cleared, and he smiled. "Cool. Let's get outta here, brother."

"I'll meet you out there," Wreck said.

Oh no he didn't.

He wasn't going to tell me how much a mistake that was. I thrust his phone out to him, and as soon as he took it, I started for the door, saying, "It's fine, Wreck. Like I said, I don't need money for that." My brother moved to the side, and I went by him, walking quickly.

"Lucas," Wreck warned.

Zion laughed. I heard them coming my way. "Brother, he's stubborn when it comes to shit like this. He won't take your money. Forget it and let's get goin'."

At the entrance to the hall, I glanced back and said, "That's right, I am stubborn, so *forget it*, Wreck." I wasn't sure when my balls had dropped and gave me a boost of confidence, but they did, and I was damn proud of them, well, me. I even said it without a blush or stumble over my words. I moved into the kitchen and grabbed out the popcorn.

"Catch ya later, Lucas," Zion said.

"You got it," I called.

"Later" was from Wreck.

"Uh-huh." When I heard the front door open and close again, I gripped the kitchen counter and sucked in a shuddering breath. "Holy shit," I whispered into the room. The adrenaline evaporated, and suddenly, my body shook with the shock of everything that just happened.

Wreck kissed me.

He *kissed me*.

Why would he do that?

More importantly, and before I got carried away with my emotions, I had to think rationally about it. Yes, the kiss was good. The best I'd had. But the look of horror from Wreck after told me he wished right away he hadn't done it. Although, why had he come here in the first place? Had he been looking for Zion and then thought screw it, it'd be fun to mess with Lucas instead?

I shook my head. That whole situation didn't make sense. What did he mean by saying I drove him insane? If anyone got to claim that, it would be me. I mean, really, he was the one who sent my mind spinning.

Then I remembered him asking if I'd seen it. He'd meant the porn on his phone. Maybe that had been playing on his mind, and he was sick of worrying if I would say anything to anyone, which could explain why he stopped by in the first place.

"But it doesn't explain the kiss," I said to myself as I stabbed my finger on the microwave buttons. Anger prompted my actions as I got out a bowl and slammed it to the counter. I stomped to the cupboard for the Nutella. I yanked it out, undid the lid, got a spoon, and dug into the thick gooey substance before shoving it in my mouth.

"Dickhead," I said around my mouthful.

He had no right stopping by and kissing me.

"Prick," I said before swallowing. When the microwave beeped, I stared at it, remembering the look on his face after that kiss.

My bottom lip trembled. I ground my teeth together, refusing to let it get to me. I wasn't ugly; at least, I didn't think I was. Yes, I was a guy, not the usual type he would make out with, but I had feelings, and he was playing with them by kissing me and then regretting it.

I had to distract myself.

I had to push that kiss to the back of my mind and lock it away.

I already knew it wouldn't happen again. I couldn't let it. I wasn't someone to try something on, even if that was what he was doing. My heart wouldn't be able to take it. I wasn't a one-night fling, and I knew that Wreck would only want that…. Who was I kidding? I didn't know him or what he was thinking.

Sighing, I finished making the popcorn and went into the living room. Sitting on the couch, I grabbed the remote and picked a movie, hoping it would have me forgetting. To start with, it worked, but of course my mind kept shoving the image of Wreck laying a demanding kiss on me, and soon my dick took notice of my thoughts. I ignored the vision and told my erection it wasn't for us to get excited over. I refused to touch myself over that man again.

I wanted to search Wreck out, kick him in the shin, and demand to know what he'd been thinking. Ideally before he wrapped his hands around my throat to choke me for kicking him in the first place. On the other hand, I wanted to bury my head in the sand and forget about it all together as there would be nothing to hope for.

I put the popcorn aside and glared at the TV. Maybe I could ask West what he would do in this situation. He could have an insight where it would ease my mind.

I looked for my phone but realized I'd left it in the bedroom. Glancing to the hall, I wished, and not for the first time, I had the power of telekinesis so I could use my mind to bring my phone to me. I didn't want to go into my room where *it* happened.

"You're being stupid," I told myself. I got up and walked down the hall right into my room. Only I couldn't see my phone. I looked over the made bed. Nothing. I searched the floor, but it wasn't there or even on my desk. Confused, I scratched at my head and thought about the last time I had it. It had been on the desk when I was studying. I moved things around and didn't let myself think of why everything was already all over the place. It wasn't because Wreck had shoved me and then looked at me like…. Nope, I wasn't thinking of any of that. What I would think of was the disappearance of my cell.

The house phone suddenly rang and, of course, the stupid movie I'd been numbing my mind to popped into my head. People had died after receiving a phone call from the murderer. Still, I went back into the living room and snatched up the receiver off the coffee table.

"Hello?"

"Lucas, it's me."

"Hi, Mom. How's everything in Australia?"

"Hot, Lucas. Damn hot."

I laughed. "Can't be as bad as here in the summer."

"I'm sure it is. But that's not what I'm ringing for. Your Dad and I are coming home for a week."

"Really? That's great, when?"

"In a couple of months. Aunt Judy is having a hysterectomy, and she'll need me to take care of her since we all know men are useless."

"Mom, you know I'm a man, right?"

"Yes, honey. I did change your diaper for years. But you have a soul, not like the rest."

Smiling, I shook my head. "Well, it will be amazing to have you both home. Will you be staying at Aunt Judy's?" Mom and Dad had sold their five-bedroom home just after they'd left, not wanting to look after such a big home when they returned. Currently, they were building a two-bedroom place not far from Zion's, but it wasn't ready yet.

"Yes, dear. Don't worry, your dad and I won't cramp your style. Speaking of, do you have someone special, honey?"

My mind took me right to an image of Wreck. I screwed that up and threw it out my ear.

"No, Mom, no one special. I'm too busy anyway with school and work."

"You have to remember, Lucas, that studying isn't everything. Learn to balance it, sweetheart. Besides, you're smart, and I'm sure you'll get good grades no matter what."

"Thanks, Mom. I'll try."

"Good. Is Zion there?"

"He's not. You can probably try and catch him on his cell."

"I'll do that, and I'll keep you posted on a set date when we'll be back. Love you, my son."

"Love you and tell Dad I said hi."

"If I have to."

Smiling, we said our goodbyes, but as soon as I hung up, my smile vanished. I blamed the stupid big biker for that. There wasn't anything I could do about it though. All I could do was take each day as it came and see what happened, but I would keep my walls up around my emotions. I wouldn't let them latch onto something that could very possibly be nothing.

Instead, I got back to finding my phone. I used the house one to ring my number. I jumped when I heard it ring close, and confusion had me dipping my brows. I walked over to the front door and saw it on the table near there.

"How?" I mumbled to myself. I pressed the End button, and my phone fell silent. I didn't pick it up though, I stared at it. How did it get down here? Did I imagine it in my room on my desk as I studied? Maybe I had, but I didn't usually put my phone on this table like Zion used it for his keys and such.

This was weird.

Finally, I put the home phone down and slowly picked up mine. I pressed the Home button. Nothing seemed different. I went through my calls, texts, apps, and photos to see if anything changed; they hadn't.

"Huh, I must have," I said to myself. Turning, I went to walk back over to the couch when my phone binged with a text; of course, it scared me. I threw it across the room and grabbed at my chest while I breathed heavily.

I really wouldn't be good if a murderer was after me. I'd just thrown my only lifeline away.

Grumbling under my breath, I stomped over, picked it up, and looked down at it.

I didn't recognize the number. I opened the message and read aloud, "Didn't mean that to happen. Won't happen again."

My stomach clenched painfully.

I didn't have to know the number. I knew who had sent it.

Wreck.

He must have gotten my phone from the bedroom to grab my number from it to send me a text of how he regretted kissing me.

I didn't need this. I was already a mess from him doing it in the first place. I didn't ask for a kiss. So what, I'd looked at his internet history. Who was to say it didn't have something to do with how I had to fix the phone? He didn't know, and he should have deleted everything if he didn't want anyone to know, and then he had the nerve to come to my place to... to... what? Kiss me? Test me? Experiment on me?

Was I supposed to reply? *"Of course, Wreck, you didn't mean to stick your tongue down my throat and wrap your arms around me. It was probably an alien taking over your body. You're too good to kiss me. I'm nothing. I'm no one. I can be used to be played with, I'm just a twenty-two-year-old fool."* I wiped roughly at my face, silently cursing at the tears.

It was fine.

Wreck was confused. He could be, but I wouldn't let him mess with me. He could do whatever he wanted. I didn't want to see him or hear from him. I wouldn't even reply to his text. I had nothing to say. That wasn't correct. I had many swear words to call him, but I refused to snap out in anger. Instead, I deleted his message.

CHAPTER SEVEN
WRECK

I was a motherfucking dickhead. As soon as I sent the text, I wanted to take it back. But I couldn't. It was too late, and I felt like a fuckhead for it. Now I stood in my room at the compound staring down at my phone, waiting for a reply, but none arrived.

Did he get my text?

Christ, had I hurt him because of the text?

"Fuckin' idiot," I cursed myself; of course I hurt him.

Lucas Storey had caught my goddamn attention from the first moment I'd seen him. Which wasn't when I'd walked into Saint's house, Lucas's blood brother. No. The first time, I'd been on a phone call outside when I saw Lucas walking down the street. He'd been mumbling to himself, waving a hand around every now and then. I couldn't really make out his features in the dark. Still, I'd hidden because his actions amused me. When he walked up to the front door and stopped there, I'd grown suspicious. Until he went back to mumbling and then rested his head against the door, like he knew it would be an effort to walk into the house, and it seemed his day hadn't been the best to begin with.

I had to hold back a laugh when Death opened the door on him, and he stumbled forward. As soon as he was through the door, I finished the call to Hailey, a woman I saw, and went inside, wanting to see what the guy would do next.

However, I wasn't prepared for the punch in the gut from actually seeing him in the light. I didn't expect his wild hair, his full lips, his slim build that matched his short stature.

It pissed me off I would notice that about the guy in the first place, so I didn't interact much with him. What had been immediately clear was that I needed to distance myself from Lucas fucking Storey. Not only was he appealing, which was motherfucking weird since I'd never felt that before for any guy, but his hems and haws and bumbling words made him goddamn cute in my eyes. Too cute since I'd snapped at the prospect over a little comment. Luckily, my brothers took it as me showing the prospect about respect. At the time, I hadn't even thought of that. I'd known Lucas had heard the prospect's words and didn't want him upset over it.

Why was he different to other guys?

Why the fuck would I notice him and his smooth skin and bright green eyes?

I went away from that first official meeting confused as fuck. I thought it was just because I'd been tired, but it seemed every damn time Saint spoke about Lucas, my ears would perk up to hear what was said.

This shit confused the hell out of me.

The second meeting, Saint had called to see if I'd wanted to hang out at his place. I needed to see if the first time was a fluke so I could shove whatever it was down the drain and get on with my days without thinking about Lucas.

Yet, when I'd found the front door unlocked, Lucas in his own bubble with music playing, it pissed me way the hell off. He was unprotected. Anyone could have walked in and harmed him in a way I knew I didn't want to see. He'd surprised me with his attitude back when I gave him a hard time. When his brother got there, I thought that Saint would help in getting him to listen, but I wasn't sure Saint had seen just how out of it Lucas became when he was studying. Then he saw it with his own eyes.

Christ, I wanted to take Lucas away from there to the compound where I knew not only I would watch him, but the brothers would as well. I fucking hated the thought of Lucas in his own goddamn world at the library or coffee shop.

He was smart. Probably smarter than all of us, so why couldn't he see the danger in getting lost around people he didn't even know?

That second encounter put Lucas on my mind more than I'd expected. I couldn't stop picturing him in his tee and sweatpants relaxing, smiling, getting angry, even when we'd all got on his case.

The thought of grabbing him, wrapping my hand in his fucking amazing curly hair, and kissing him again hit me hard, shocking me to the core.

My attention to Lucas was a need to look out for him for Saint's sake. It wasn't though. And I called bullshit right away.

And then I was left with why him?

I'd never, fucking *never*, been into a guy before.

What made him catch my attention?

Frustrated, I scrubbed a hand over my face and kicked out at my bed. The mattress tipped up and then back down.

I'd fucked things up. Massively.

But it was probably for the best. I couldn't be interested in a guy. Women were my thing. I loved fucking them.

Then why had I sought Lucas out after I'd noticed what had been in my internet history? I'd forgotten to delete it—a stupid move on my part, especially after Lucas had had it. Hell, if I'd been in the same boat, I would have done the same and looked through his phone. He would have seen it, so I'd just had to question him about it. I'd planned to play it off as one of the brothers fucking with me and putting that on there, but as soon as I saw him and he started his hemming and hawing, acting like he didn't see shit I couldn't.

Fucking foolish move admitting to Lucas how he drove me insane.

Christ, I didn't even know if I was someone he'd go for, but it'd been too late. I'd had him in my arms, my brain telling me to feel things out, see if it was just a damn phase or some shit. But when I had him there, in my arms, with my lips on his, and I felt him start to pull back, I didn't want to let go. I took his mouth, and he seemed to like it. He grabbed on instead of shoving me off.

That fucking kiss.

That goddamn kiss.

It'd be seared into my head for the rest of my life.

I thought it'd be weird kissing a guy, but in the moment, it hadn't been. Then I royally screwed things up when I freaked out, hearing Saint's voice. I'd seen the flash of pain on Lucas's features, and my gut had twisted. It still did each time the moment ran through my mind.

Then I went and royally screwed up more by sending that text in a moment of fear.

Fear because he was a guy.

Fear if anyone found out and the shit we'd get.

Fear over liking it.

Fear over wanting more and what that meant for me.

I wasn't willing to change my life. I liked my damn life as it was. Lucas couldn't just rock into it and have my head and body switching things up.

He couldn't.

So it was good I'd sent the text. He'd get the picture. That was if he got the text. No, he did. I'd stolen his phone off his desk when I'd stood and managed to get his number in my phone before I hit the front door. He would have since seen it.

Then why did I wish he hadn't?

It was a dick move.

I should have just left it alone and never seen him again. I knew it'd be hard, but he'd managed to dodge me after seeing what was on my phone. It brought me back to wondering why he'd dodged me? My lips tipped up. If I was to guess, it would be because he was scared he'd crack under pressure and admit everything.

It would have been good to see, but then I wouldn't have felt his sweet, plump lips on mine.

Groaning, I dropped my head and rubbed at the back of my neck.

I had to forget him.

A knock sounded on my door. The compound was in full swing of a party happening in the common room, but I wasn't in the mood.

Opening the door, I found Hailey on the other side. I knew after having her more than twice she would think we were something. We weren't, and it was going to suck telling her that.

"Hey, baby," she cooed, stepping close and rubbing her hands up my chest. "Miss you out there. You going to join the party, or do you wanna make your own in here?"

She would be a good distraction.

But who was I kidding? Even as I stared down at her big tits, my dick didn't even take notice of the chance to get off. If anything, he was damn asleep. Unless I thought of Lucas.

Jesus Christ, my dick throbbed from only the thought of his name. If it could speak, I was sure it'd be saying, "Huh? Lucas is here? Where?"

I'd also be a bigger asshole than I was if I gave her something she thought she wanted and made her think there was an us.

Fuck my life.

I lay my hands over hers. "Darlin'." Her eyes narrowed. "It's been good, but it can't go on. I'm not looking for an old lady."

"Wreck, do not do this."

"Hailey…."

"No. You want me. I know you do. I would make a great old lady. Head whenever you want. I'd even let you fuck me in front of your brothers."

"See, that's the thing. When I get an old lady, which won't be any time soon, I won't want anyone to touch them, look at them." I could see the stubborn glint in her eyes. "Hailey, you'll find someone that's it for you, but it ain't me. Still, if you ever need anythin', you know I'm here. Yeah?"

"I'm needing now, Wreck." She tried to slide her hands up further, but I held them in place.

"You ain't gonna get from me anymore, darlin'."

She smirked. "I'm sure I could persuade you." I didn't expect her hand to drop, but it did, and next she cupped my junk. "See, baby, you're on the road to getting hard for me."

Problem was, it wasn't for her I had a chub.

Fucking Lucas.

Grabbing her hand, I gently shoved her back. "Not happenin', Hailey. Don't make this any harder than it already is."

She laughed. "But that's what I'm aiming for."

I shook my head and crossed my arms over my chest. She wasn't getting anything else off me, not until I had my head on straight, and even then, she wouldn't because she was after one thing. She wanted to be someone's old lady. It would never be with me. I could handle her for a few hours if an orgasm came at the end, but not all the damn time. Made me sound like a prick, but she'd been willing for me to stick my dick in her, and I made sure she was satisfied in the end.

"We had something special starting, Wreck. How can you do this to me?"

"You saw more than what I was offerin'."

She planted her hands on her hips, and I knew shit was about to get ugly. "You could just tell me the truth, that you're having problems sexually since the last time you didn't want to fuck either. I'll be sure to tell the other girls to steer clear because your dick isn't working."

The last time was when I saw Lucas sitting in a café with a guy I didn't know. They'd been laughing, smiling, and touching. I hadn't meant to go up to their table, but I felt I had to, for Saint's sake. I had to make sure Lucas was safe with whoever he was with. I'd hated the guy he was with right away. It wasn't until I heard they were friends that the burn inside me calmed.

I was supposed to take Hailey to the compound and fuck her. I couldn't. My head wasn't in the right space, so I dropped her home. However, before she got out of the car, she tried to rub me over. My dick didn't show interest. I pretended I wasn't feeling well. She didn't know I went back to the compound, got hard instantly when I thought of Lucas, and tugged one out.

Still, she didn't need to spread shit about me. I took a step toward her. Glaring, I told her, quietlike, "If anything gets around, I'll know where it came from, and the brothers and I will make your life hell. Do not start this crap, Hailey. Get me?"

"Yes," she whispered right away.

"Good, now get."

She turned and ran down the hall.

I rubbed a hand over my head. I hadn't wanted it to go that way. She'd been an all right chick, but she pushed me. She went too far, and there was only so much I could take.

No one threatened me.

I'd put up with enough in my life and wouldn't have some woman try that shit on me. I was older, somewhat wiser, and ever since I grew into the man I was and got out of the house I'd been in —when I couldn't take care of myself and had to take the beatings, the belittling—I refused to let anyone do it to me again.

No matter who it was.

Sighing, I stepped back into my room and closed the door behind me, locking it. I went back to my phone on the bed, picked it up, and checked to see if Lucas had replied.

There was nothing.

I didn't blame him. He was being the better person. Still, I'd hoped he'd given me his attitude or fought for something from me.

Fucking hell, what was I thinking? Why did I want him to fight when I refused to do it myself?

I didn't need this new development in my life.

I had to forget about Lucas Storey.

What I wished the damn most was knowing why he was different. Why he appealed to me when it'd always been women, their curves, their tits, their tight, wet, hot hole I could slip into.

"Fuck my life," I muttered, because all I wanted to do was slip into Lucas.

I huffed out a laugh. Never did I imagine some guy's ass would turn me on, but it did. Hell, I'd even checked it out, thinking of taking a handful to see what it felt like.

Would his small body be able to take mine?

Shit, I had to stop thinking about it.

I needed a drink and to be around my brothers. They'd keep my mind off things.

My phone rang and my damn heart gave a little jerk. I grabbed it, noticed it wasn't Lucas's number, and disappointment had me tightening my grip on my phone and clipping out, "What?"

"Where the fuck are you?" came Death's voice.

"In my room."

He chuckled. "You with a piece of ass?"

The only ass I wanted I didn't really want. Fuck, did that even make sense? "No," I bit out.

Death snorted. "Sounds like you need some though. Want me to send Hailey down there? She's out here looking for some. All over Saint at the moment."

"I sent her packin'. Don't need her back."

"Ah, no wonder you're uptight. What about Tesha?"

"Brother, I don't need pussy. There a reason why you called?"

"Yeah, the prez and VP just got back. Callin' for church in half an hour."

"I'll be there. They look all right?"

"In good spirits, so it should be good."

I grunted and then ended the call. Country and State were the president and vice president of the club. They'd been on the road for the last month, setting up a new charter in the town over. It would be good to have them back, and they might even need someone to go back there to watch things. I could be that man. It meant getting out of town and away from Lucas, which could be good for both of us.

CHAPTER EIGHT
WRECK

J was weak. Country hadn't needed anyone to go back to the other club, so I threw myself into work, club business, and drinking. How I turned out weak was because it'd only been a couple of weeks, and already, I wanted my fill of Lucas.

It was like he was a beacon of light in a dark day, which sounded fucking pathetic and weird since I hardly knew him. But it was just how he acted, his looks, how I never knew what would fall out of his mouth…. It all drew me in and made me smile.

I was also weak because I sat on Saint's couch, pretending to watch a basketball game with him while waiting for Lucas to get home from classes.

It was fucking stupid for me being there, but when Saint suggested it, I was the first to say I'd come over. I was the first because I didn't want to go another day without seeing him.

How fucking strange was that?

I wanted to see a guy for a reason I never thought would be possible with me. I wanted to see him because I liked hearing him, I liked looking at him, and being around him.

Jesus motherfucking Christ, I sounded like I'd lost my balls and grew a pussy.

Saint nudged my knee with his. "What's been up with you lately?"

"Nothin'."

"Wreck, you're pissed more these days. Is it about Hailey? You pissed I took her to bed? 'Cause you can have her back. That bitch is clingy."

I snorted. "Told you before, I don't want anythin' to do with her. I also warned you how she was—only after becomin' an old lady."

"Shit. I know, but I didn't think one night, one fuckin' night would have her thinkin' about weddin' bells. Though, Pog seems keen to lock her down."

"True." Pog and Hailey had been inseparable for the last week. Only four days after Saint had her, but Pog didn't care. He was infatuated with her. We also knew he wasn't the type to break her heart. Though if she broke him, we'd have words. Maybe I needed to word her up in case she was playing him.

The front door opened, my gut gave a lurch, and my pulse took off. Lucas stepped in with his head down, calling, "How come you get to leave the front door unlocked, but I can't?" He mustn't have noticed my bike out front. Probably in his own world.

Saint laughed. "That's because I can kick someone's ass."

Lucas dropped his bag and bent over to go through it for something.

"Pfft, please, I can beat someone up."

Saint chuckled at his brother.

I thinned my lips, taking in the view. My dick seemed to like it as well. Jesus, that was a mind fuck. But he had a nice ass that was encased in cotton. On top, as he straightened with books in his arms, I noticed he wore a hoody. It was baggy on his small body.

He looked up and noticed me sitting there watching him. The books dropped to the floor, his face went bright red, and he quickly grabbed them up. I could see the tightness to his jaw.

He cleared his throat, stood again, and said, "Ah, yeah, hey, um, Wreck. Didn't see you there." He laughed nervously. I liked him nervous around me. "So, um…." He licked his lips. Was he trying to tease me? I knew he wouldn't be. His mouth was probably dry from the fear of seeing the one man I knew he wouldn't want to see.

Well, he shouldn't have been so tempting.

Fuck.

He started toward the kitchen. "My turn to make dinner, so, um, I'll get right on it. Night—I mean bye."

He'd nearly made it, but then Saint called, "Hey, don't rush off. How'd lunch go with that guy?"

That guy?

There was a guy?

What fucking guy?

I dug my fingers into the couch but kept my stare on the TV and not Lucas. I didn't want him to notice I was pissed he'd been out with a guy. I didn't have a right to be pissed. I didn't own Lucas.

Fucking stupid head. Fucking stupid body. Why the hell did they have to react to a guy? To *this* guy? To Saint's younger brother. Saint would have my balls if he knew I was thinking of his brother. Shit, there were twelve years between us. I shouldn't even have been thinking about a guy that age. A guy in the first place.

"Ah, good," he squeaked. I would have found it cute, but I didn't, not with the thought of him with another guy swirling around in my head.

"Then I don't need to hunt him down?"

I did.

Lucas laughed, but it was forced. "No." He clapped his hands. "Dinner. I'll get it. Now."

Saint's brows dipped. He looked over his shoulder to Lucas, but his brother was already clattering around in the kitchen. Saint glanced back to me. "Do you think he's telling the truth?"

"About what?" I growled.

Saint's brow rose at my tone.

"Sorry, just had a shit day."

"Yeah, all right. But about that guy? That he had a good time?"

"Dunno." I shrugged, even when it hurt to move because my body was tense.

"I can hear you," Lucas called. "Remember what I said about my private life? You don't need to talk about it."

"Fine," Saint called. I went back to looking at the TV. I didn't watch it, just stared as I listened to Lucas in the kitchen. He hummed when he cooked. Yet another damn cute thing he did. Would it ever stop? I was sure he did this stuff to get me to like him more.

It was some time later when Lucas called, "Dinner."

Shit, I had to go.

Standing, I said, "I'll catch up later."

A throat cleared. I glanced at Lucas. His hair was tied up, and I wanted to reach out to let the curls loose. His cheeks were tinged pink, and he looked everywhere but at me as he stumbled through, "Ah, there's, um, yeah, enough." He shrugged, turned, and then went to the table.

Saint's hand slapped to my shoulder. "Brother, when you taste the shit Lucas cooks, there's a chance you'll want to kidnap him."

Was that a choice?

Lucas coughed, then choked. "Ha, it's not that good."

We went to the table and on it sat marinated lamb chops, mashed potatoes, and a bowl of mixed vegetables.

Goddamn. "Looks good," I said gruffly. I hadn't had a home-cooked meal in a damn long time. Saint was right. I'd already imagined kidnapping Lucas, but after this, I'd want to keep him.

"Thanks," Lucas whispered. I took a seat opposite him, while Saint sat at the end of the table. We piled our plates. Actually, Saint and I did; Lucas only had two chops and a small number of vegetables.

"You should eat more," I said before thinking. Lucas's fork stopped halfway to his mouth as he stared at me with what could be shock.

Saint chuckled. "He's just a wittle boy still."

Lucas glared at him. "If you want my food again, you won't say that. Ever."

"Got it." Saint grinned.

"Saint ever cook?" I asked Lucas.

He glanced at me and then down to his food. "No. Not if we want to live. On his days of cooking, it's always takeout, which is why I try to cook on my days."

"How's that gonna go when you start med school?"

His wide eyes lifted to me. I'd heard Saint and Kylo talking about his degree. Didn't he think I'd be interested? Lucas straightened, cleared his throat, and then shrugged. "I'll make it work, even with the crazy hours."

"Thank fuck," Saint said, rubbing his stomach.

"What made you want to be a doctor?" I asked, and Saint gave me a funny look, which I ignored.

"It's always appealed to me. Helping people," Lucas said in a soft voice as he used his fork to play with his food.

"What else do you like to do?" I asked, and it was Saint's turn to pause with his fork in his hand. I ignored him again, let him think what he wanted because I could easily say he was Saint's brother and wasn't it good to get to know him?

Lucas took a sip of his can of soda. "Um… stuff. What's your real name?"

I smirked but wiped it away. He was deflecting, but at least he was asking me things. "Wade."

"How did you get Wreck?" He glanced at his brother, and I wanted to punch Saint for taking his gaze away. "In fact, how did you get your club name? You're no Saint." Lucas smiled.

Saint chuckled and winked, pointing his fork at his brother. "You know it. I got the name because I look like a saint with my charming self. Little do they know I can turn dark in a second."

"You? Dark?"

Saint reached out and patted Lucas's arm. "You just keep believin' I'm the awesome older brother."

Lucas laughed. "Awesome? Yeah, okay."

Why did I fucking feel left out? It irritated me enough to interrupt with "My club name is Wreck because I crashed my ride when I was a prospect."

"Heard about that," Saint said. "You wrecked it completely."

I nodded. "Yep. Was lucky I only got a broken arm from it." Lucas made a noise and I asked, "What was that?"

His eyes flashed. "What?" He actually looked beside him and over his shoulder.

"That noise. What was with the noise about my accident or my club name?"

His face turned red. "Nothing."

"Oh, it was somethin'," Saint said with a chuckle. "He wouldn't turn that red if it wasn't." Saint cursed. "Shit, don't kick me, bro."

"It was nothing," Lucas said again.

"Lucas," I said low.

"Anyway, how about the weather?" He tried to change the subject, but I wasn't having it.

"Lucas," I growled.

"Would you look at the time. It's getting late." He stood.

"Lucas," I clipped, leaning forward in my chair.

Lucas groaned, ran a hand down his face, and said, "Fine." He sat back down, his eyes to the table. "I, ah… just thought that… I mean your club name… I thought it, um, meant something else."

"What?"

He scrubbed a hand over his mouth and mumbled behind it.

"I didn't catch that."

He glared over at me. "That you wrecked women in bed," he blurted, then shoveled a mouthful of vegetables in his mouth.

I dipped my brows, confused. "In what way?"

Saint snorted but didn't say anything.

Lucas coughed and thumped his fist against his chest. "You know."

"No, I don't."

I wasn't sure if it was a good way or bad.

He rolled his eyes, which dropped back to his plate. "In a good way, where they wouldn't want to leave."

Suddenly I felt like I wanted to puff my chest out. If he thought I was good in bed, it was a good thing. Did it mean he wanted to try?

Not that we would.

We couldn't.

Why did I even want to see if I could wreck him in bed?

Fuck.

Saint slapped the table, laughing. "Shit, that's a good one. I gotta tell the other brothers. Hell, it could be true, right, Wreck?"

I grunted. I didn't have anything to say, too worried I'd admit to wanting to try it with his brother.

"See, you shouldn't have pushed. Now it's all awkward." Lucas glared. Had he been thinking what I had? Fuck, I hoped he wasn't picturing me with women. Christ, I didn't even think how he would have seen the women's photos on my phone. I'd just saved them in case any caused trouble down the track, and also so I remembered who to avoid.

Hell, now I felt sick because he'd seen them all.

Motherfucking hell, why did I care so much?

"What classes did you have today?" I asked, instead of admitting I'd made the moment awkward.

Lucas seemed to relax into the conversation and practically shined talking about his classes. It was good to see. I had a feeling he hated me for being a dick, but he was still willing to share stuff about himself. It showed me he was a damn good person. Not only that, but I was interested to know everything I could about him.

Was I just digging my own grave of hell?

Why was I still interested when I'd talked myself into not trying anything with him?

Because he was different.

Different to any guy and different to any woman I'd had before.

Definitely different in a good way.

I was fucked. This shit was going to mess me up and confuse me more. I thought it'd help me in a way I'd notice it was all a phase or some shit, but it wasn't. I could watch and listen to Lucas for fucking hours, and that was just crazy.

No one had brought this reaction out of me before.

Did I want to lose that feeling?

Could I risk starting something?

I glanced at Saint, who was laughing at something. He could possibly kill me for even thinking any of this shit, but it wasn't like I could help it. My brain had been recharged in a way it never had before, ever since I'd set eyes on Lucas.

Hell, what in the fuck was I going to do?

Did I walk away or take what I wanted?

The next day I was still thinking about when I'd walked into the house and saw Wreck sitting in the living room. My emotions had volleyed between anger and nerves. Why had he been there? How dare he be there in the first place, especially after what he'd said to me! He didn't want anything to do with me, so why had he come to the house where he knew I lived? Unless Zion asked him...? Could he have said no to my brother's invite? I was sure he could have thought of something.

For the first time in my life, I'd wanted to punch someone in the balls.

Then I had to open my big mouth and offer him to stay for dinner. Even my mind had battled itself. The left half told me how handsome he looked, and how it would be good to lick him, marking him as mine. While the right part had me near believing poison was the right option.

It was all too confusing. What made it more so were all the questions he'd thrown at me. Why did he care to know anything about me after telling me I was a mistake?

How was I supposed to work him out when he changed his

ways? He gave me mixed signals. It was like he had two personalities—one good, one a douche.

Shaking my head, I went back to work on the Xbox in front of me before my boss yelled at me for slacking. I'd decided I didn't want to know Wreck's intentions. As far as I was concerned, he didn't exist in my world any longer.

Besides, I had a date to get ready for.

I would push Wreck to the back of my mind and put all my attention on to Gregory. I'd promised myself. I still couldn't believe when Gregory asked me out again, and I'd told him I was in a mixed emotional state over another guy, that he still wanted to see me outside of college. Of course, I'd asked him a million times if he was sure, because I couldn't promise him anything. He'd smiled shyly and said yes each time.

It wasn't until I was back in my room after work that I regretted my choice, but only because I was a bundle of nerves.

Standing in my black boxers, I shot off a text to Kylo and West. They met each other a few days ago and got along really well. West finally understood how easy it was to become friends with Kylo's happy attitude.

Me: What does a guy wear on a date where he's not sure if he should be going so he doesn't want to lead him on, but could probably handle a kiss in the end to see how it goes?

Kylo: A mankini.

West: Jeans, sweater, and take a condom in case. Though Kylo's suggestion would make me laugh.

Kylo: Exactly. Call us if you do so we can watch.

Me: It's freezing out. It'll look like I have a vagina.

Kylo: Take a jacket for over the top ;)

West: Lol, and don't forget your rain boots.

Me: You guys are such good help (not) However, I think I'll go with jeans, tee, and jacket.

Kylo: Boring, but fine. Make sure you have fun.

West: Yes, forget that other guy and give this one a chance.

Kylo: Other guy? WHO?

Dang it. West didn't know I hadn't told Kylo about Wreck. I should have warned West not to say anything. I hadn't even thought of it since West didn't bring Wreck up in front of Kylo when they'd met.

West: My bad. It was no one. I was thinking of someone else.

Kylo: Bullshit. Now I have to know.

I needed time. I couldn't have Kylo knowing just yet. Yes, there was nothing to know, but I feared he would say something to Wreck by accident. I didn't want Kylo to go up against Wreck.

Me: I'll tell you in person. Just not yet. Please.

Kylo: Fine. This shit sounds juicy though.

Me: I better get ready. Talk soon.

Kylo: Later.

West: Bye, enjoy your night. There was a moment, and then I got a private message from West out of the group one. **West: I'm so sorry about that. I didn't even think.**

Me: It's okay, I would have told him eventually. Maybe.

West: I'm sure he'll keep it to himself if you ask.

Me: I think so too.

Actually, I prayed he would, and I couldn't expect him to drop it. I would be the same if the shoe were on the other foot. Dropping my phone, I quickly got dressed and headed back out into the living room just as there was a knock on the front door.

"Coming," I called. I put on my shoes and went to unlock and open the front door only to freeze. "Zion's not here," I blurted quickly and glanced around him to see if Gregory had arrived. He'd wanted to pick me up. I told him I'd meet him at the restaurant, but he wanted the destination to be a surprise. I caved. I shouldn't have because now there was a big problem at the front door.

Wreck's lips twitched. "He'll be here soon."

"Then… ah, maybe come back?"

Wreck crossed his arms over his wide chest encased in a black long-sleeve Henley and his club vest. I was surprised his teeth weren't chattering; it was freezing.

His chin tipped up. "Cold as shit, you gonna let me in?"

"Um… can I say no?"

"No." He smirked.

Crappity crap. "I mean, you're right. It is cold. You better get your bike out of this weather."

"I drove." His eyes narrowed. "You tryin' to get rid of me?"

"No," I squeaked.

"Lucas?" was called from behind Wreck. "Everything okay?"

Damn my luck.

Wreck shifted to the side. I plastered on a bright smile that could have looked a little crazed and said, "Hey, Gregory. Ah, yes, everything is good."

"Who the fuck is this?" Wreck demanded, his tone all growly and cute.

No. No, it wasn't cute because he would have Gregory peeing himself in seconds if I didn't get out of here.

"None of your business," I shouted, slapped a hand over my mouth, and then took it away to blurt, "Gregory, I just have to get my jacket and we can go." I went to turn around, but my upper arm was seized. I tensed and glanced back to see Wreck scowling down at Gregory.

"Get."

"W-What?" Gregory stuttered, his eyes wide.

"Wreck, stop it. It's okay, Gregory. He's a friend of my brother's just looking out for me. I won't be a second." I pulled enough that Wreck followed me inside. Unfortunately, he slammed the door in Gregory's face.

Since he still had a hold of my arm, he spun me to face him and backed me up until the backs of my legs hit the couch.

"Stop it," I told him, if only my voice didn't make it sound like I enjoyed being crowded by Wreck. Stupid traitor.

His hand dropped away, and two fingers touched under my chin, gently pushing my head back so he could have my gaze. "Who. Is. He?"

My heart tried to jump out of my body, and it felt as if my pulse wanted to beat closer to him, but I was miffed he thought he had the right to ask. Even if he was doing it because I was his biker brother's brother.

After unhinging my grinding teeth, I snarked, "None of your business."

His nostrils flared, his eyes flashed, and he dipped his head lower. "It is."

I shook my head. I needed to get away from him. He had no right to play me because my heart was telling me he was asking because he was interested in me. However, he'd made clear he wasn't.

I pressed my hands into his stomach, his firm, moan-worthy stomach and pushed back. He didn't move. Stupid, large muscular man.

Since I couldn't move the brick, I shifted to the side, grabbed my jacket off the back of the couch, and turned to him, hugging the jacket close as if it could protect me—from him or from me, jumping him.

In a quiet voice, I asked, "Why do you care? Why do you want to know? You're not my brother, and you don't need to look out for me for Zion. I'm living my own life doing what I want. I don't have anyone I need to justify to. Now, if you'll excuse me, I have somewhere to go."

At my first question, he looked to the ground, and his jaw had clenched so tightly I was surprised he hadn't shattered his teeth by the end.

I made my way to the front door and held my hand on it. I hoped Wreck would call me back, but when he didn't, my belly dropped to my toes. Nodding to myself, I opened the door and stepped out, forcing a smile.

"Sorry about that. My brother had his friends look out for me ever since I moved in. Since Wreck didn't know you, he kind of went overboard with the whole protective step-in brother act."

Gregory grinned. "It's okay. But… you still want to do this, right?"

I slipped on my jacket. "Yes, of course." *No, not really.* But just because my mood had plummeted, I refused to let it stop me from giving this a chance. Just maybe Gregory could, in fact, sweep me off my feet.

The night wasn't too bad. By the time Gregory walked me to the front door at the end of the date, I had a smile on my face. I'd managed to forget about Wreck because Gregory made sure of it. He took me to a restaurant where there was a show as well. It was that entertaining and I had such good company, everything just fell away.

"Thank you again. I had an amazing time," I said, turning to him on the front porch.

His smile almost seemed shy as he kicked at the ground. "You're welcome. I'm glad you could make it."

"So am I."

He lifted his brown gaze to mine. "Does it mean you'd want to do it again?"

"I'm not sure when. I have a few exams I have to study up for, but I'd like to."

Now his smile was wide. "Great. Don't worry, I understand about studying. Maybe we could do it together one time?"

"Sounds like a plan."

"Good." He nodded, still smiling. "Would… can I kiss you?"

My stomach gave off a little pitter-patter feeling. "Yes."

He stepped closer, his hands going to my shoulders, while I put mine on his hips. We were about the same height, so it was good when all he had to do was lean in and press his lips to mine. It was tender, sweet even.

Light suddenly shined over the both of us.

Startled, we pulled away, and both looked at the front door. In it stood a smiling Zion. "Sorry about that. Just heading out to grab some more beer."

"T-That's all right," Gregory stammered, blushing tomato red. I knew my cheeks were flaming as well, maybe just not as much. "I b-better get going."

"You sure?" Zion asked. "You can come on in."

"Oh, n-no, thank you. I have to get up early."

Gregory's stumble over his words with Wreck and Zion had me thinking about why he didn't do it with me. He was shy with me, but not enough to freak out like he was.

"All right then." Zion's hand shot out. "Since my baby bro isn't forthcoming with introductions, I guess I'll do it. Name's Zion, Lucas's brother."

I hadn't even thought to. I was still annoyed he'd opened the door in the first place. I'd hoped to enjoy the kiss… see if it took off, or was the interruption a blessing in disguise? Why was I suddenly doubting it?

Slowly, Gregory took Zion's hand, and he gulped. "Gregory. Nice to m-meet you."

"You too. Well, I'll be off. Wreck's inside, and Death's on his way over with Quake. We'll keep it down. Don't stress, bro." Zion patted my arm as he walked by. I would have said something if I wasn't stuck on Wreck being inside the house on his own.

I didn't want to walk in there knowing he was there.

Maybe I could army crawl in, and he wouldn't notice me. I would even try an army roll if I thought it would work.

Great, now all I could think about was Wreck in the house, so when Gregory called my name, I jumped like a little girl.

"Yes?"

He smiled. "I'll see you at school?"

I nodded. "That would be great, and we'll do a study date soon."

"Okay, thanks again for coming tonight."

"Thanks for inviting me." I grinned. He shot me a half-wave, turned, and made his way back to the car. I stayed on the front porch until he pulled away with a second wave, which I returned.

Then I thought I could just wait outside until my brother got back or Death and Quake arrived. I would have if I wasn't starting to get chilled to the bone. Sighing, I rubbed a hand across my chest, but it didn't help my fast-beating heart. I went through the front door quietly, kind of hoping Wreck had somehow magically fallen asleep.

After closing it, I turned and found him standing just behind me. I screamed and then covered my mouth with both hands.

Wreck's lips twitched. I glared at them, deciding it was safer than making eye contact. "Don't ever do that again." I kicked off my shoes and removed my jacket before walking around him. "I'm… yeah, ah, tired. Goodnight."

His footfalls sounded loud as they followed me down the hall. I glanced back; his eyes were to the floor. Maybe he was just walking this way to go to the bathroom. People had to pee.

I passed the bathroom and opened my bedroom door. Before I could close it, a hand landed on it.

Licking my dry lips nervously, I looked up and asked in a soft voice, "Do you need something?"

His eyes ran over my face. "Did he kiss you?" he bit out.

My heart stumbled over a beat. He couldn't ask me that. He had no right to ask me that. Why was he even asking me?

"I… you…. I don't understand this," I admitted.

His jaw clenched. "Answer me."

"Why?"

His nostrils flared. "I need to know."

"Again, why?"

"Are you seeing him again?"

"He goes to my college," I said in the way of an answer that wasn't really one.

He made a noise deep in the back of his throat. "Are you dating him?"

"We're getting to know one another." Which was true.

"He isn't for you," he stated.

I jerked my head back in shock. "What do you mean?" I shook my head. "Actually, I don't need to know because it doesn't matter."

"You need someone else," he clipped.

I threw my hands up, dropping my jacket in the process. "Who? And I swear to God, if you say anyone but him, I will kick you in the balls. I've never done it to anyone, but I'm this close, Wreck." I held up my finger and thumb to show him I was inches away from destroying his manhood with my foot. "This close," I snapped. I shook my head, groaned, and rubbed a hand over my head. "You know what, I don't need this. You kiss me, you freak out, you come back into my life, which I understand is probably because you're friends with my brother, but if we have to see each other, we don't need moments like this. Please, you're hurting my head." *And heart.* "We need to stay out of each other's way." I stopped short as this was seriously messing with me, and I was sure murder would eventually be in the cards.

"I don't—"

"Yo" was called when the front door suddenly opened. I peeked around Wreck to see Death and Quake step into the house. "What's goin' on?"

"Nothin'," Wreck snarled before turning and making his way back down the hall, then into the living room. Quake followed after him after he tipped his chin at me.

Death stared down the hall at me. "You okay, kid?"

"Fine. All good." I rolled my eyes. "Wreck was just asking me something about his phone." I shot him two thumbs-up. "All's peachy." I went too far; he still looked suspicious.

"Right," he drew out. "You comin' out for a drink?"

"No, thanks. I've got class in the morning. Have a good night though."

Death nodded but said no more. With a smile, I closed my bedroom door and leaned against it. I couldn't believe I'd said all that to Wreck. I wished I'd gotten to hear what he was going to reply with, but at least he knew where I stood. At least, I thought he did.

CHAPTER TEN
LUCAS

Sleep was a struggle since the night Gregory had taken me out. Actually, the whole week had gone by in slow motion, where I wasn't sure if I was living or not. I put it down to the lack of sleep. It wasn't only because of Wreck and his actions that confused me. It wasn't. I refused to think of the man. Classes were, for once, kicking my butt as well. Something Mitch "Dick-face" Henry thought was hilarious since, for the first time, he got a higher score on a test than me. I was sure he thought it had to do with the other two threatening notes I got, but it wasn't because I just found them ridiculous. So then, I reminded him, as I left class on Friday, that he shouldn't act too cocky since it was the first and last time. It didn't stop him gloating some more though.

I was just glad the weekend had finally arrived. I was going to laze around in between studying. I didn't have work that weekend since every fourth weekend I got off. I'd just exited the shower when there was a knock on the bathroom door.

"Lucas," Zion called.

"Yeah?" He was probably heading out and wanted to tell me. We'd both had a day at home and did hardly anything. Except I hit the books every now and then.

"Hurry up."

Pausing as I dried my head, I moved the towel to my chest and asked, "Why?"

"Family night at the compound. You're comin' with."

Oh no I wasn't.

"Ah, no, thank you though."

"Lucas, family night. You're comin'."

"I can't. I have studying to do."

"I knew I should have told you after I got you in the car," he complained.

With the towel around my waist, I walked to the door and opened it. "You should have, but I probably wouldn't have gotten out of the car afterward."

"Why? You worried about the brothers and what they'll think? You've met some of them, and I know they'll have your back. You got nothin' to fear. Come on, bro, do it for me. I wanna show you my world. Meet the rest of my brothers."

And now I felt guilty for not wanting to. But really, the only reason I didn't want to was because of the chance of seeing Wreck. I hadn't seen him all week, and it had been for the best as even though he wasn't in front of me, he was still on my mind…. Wait, I wasn't admitting that to myself. I couldn't exactly tell Zion I didn't want to go because of Wreck either; he'd be in my business in a quick flash.

I sighed. "Fine. I'll go get dressed."

"Great." He grinned and moved out of my way.

Already my nerves kicked in as I dressed in jeans, boots, a tee, and then a black hoodie over it, which had an outline of Mario on the back of it in red. My stomach wouldn't stop twisting, and I worried I would bring the pizza I'd consumed earlier up. I stuck my shaky hand in the pockets of my hoodie when I walked back down the hall.

Zion stood from the couch. "Awesome, let's go."

I nodded.

In the car, Zion rambled on for the both of us since he knew I'd be just about crapping myself about the party, but also the number of people, and then there was Wreck. I had my fingers crossed he wouldn't be there.

"Lucas, what do you think?"

I blinked a few times. "Sorry, what?"

He laughed. "I knew you'd be nervous, but hell, bro, you look like you might piss yourself."

"It could be a possibility. Maybe you should just take me home. I don't want to embarrass you."

He shook his head. "You won't, and we're nearly there anyway."

Dang it all. I glanced out the window. I could jump out of the car and make a run for it. Then again, I didn't want to worry Zion.

Shaking my head, I asked, "What did you say before?"

"I was thinking of an idea for the Polished Pussy and wanted your opinion on it."

"Hit me," I said, turning in my seat to give him my full attention.

"All right, be honest with me. What do you think if we added guys to the place?"

My brows dipped. "What do you mean? Don't guys already go there?"

"Not like that, but there could be a market for women who want a hookup for the night. Even gay men who want company but don't want to find it on a sleazy datin' site. Our place ain't sleazy. We find the best of the fuckin' best, and we make sure all employees are takin' care of."

"Aren't there already guy prostitutes out there?"

"Yeah, but they won't be like ours. Ours will cater to women and men."

"It might be hard finding men who switch both ways. How many would you be wanting?"

"Ten, I reckon. But what do you think?"

I shrugged. "I think it's always good to find ways to branch the business out. Men aren't the only ones wanting a no-hassle hookup even when paying for it. There's a lot of married women out there who are very happy in their marriage, but when it comes to their sex life, they're unsatisfied. They don't want to cheat, and you could do group sessions where the husband can come along as well so they can watch and get off in their own way." I shrugged again. "Sorry, I was just running with a thought."

He pulled into a fenced-off area. "That's a fuckin' great idea. I'll run it by the brothers, and we'll get shit set up on the website." After he parked and turned off the car, he gently punched me in the arm. "Thanks, bro. Now, let's get in there and have some fun." He opened his door and got out.

Before he could close it, I called, "But not too much fun, right? We won't stay long, right?"

Zion just laughed as he shut his door. Slowly, I got out of my side and met him at the front of the car. When I noticed he didn't lock up, I mentioned it to him. He grinned. "No one would dare take shit from it or come into our territory to even try to take it. Besides, got brothers on guard. Yo, Quake, Bobo," Zion called into the darkness.

"Hey" came a reply, and it sounded like Quake. I knew it was him when he added, "Hey, little Saint."

"Hi." I waved and probably did it in the wrong direction since chuckles sounded next.

Zion's arm wound around my shoulders, and he pulled me along. "Don't worry about Bobo answering. He doesn't like to talk." I nodded and still found myself waving again. More laughter followed. God, I was an idiot.

Already I could hear the music blaring and people talking. I wanted to pull my hood up and hide.

"You won't leave me, right?"

At the double doors, he shook me from side to side with his arm still around my shoulders. "Don't stress, Lucas. Promise I won't leave your side unless the prospect, Death, or Wreck is there."

Oh, snap, Wreck *was* going to be there.

"A-Ah, okay."

He dropped his arm, grabbed the handle of the door, and opened it. He waved me in, but I shook my head. Zion shook his head, smiling, and stepped into the room. Cheers erupted, and they were so loud, my anxiety jumped, and I took a step back.

Zion glanced back at me. He rolled his eyes, grabbed my wrist, and pulled me into the room. Death was there, and between him and my brother, they introduced me to so many others that there was no way I'd remember their names, but they all seemed friendly enough.

Finally, we'd found a quiet corner, and my eyes had been opened to Zion's world like it never had before. There were so many members in this club, so many different men had joined. I'd seen old, young, tall, short, skinny, fat, hot, smoking hot, sweet, scary, angry…. It was a little mind-blowing. The women ranged from different looks as well. There weren't as many as the men, but I'd been told by Death that was because not all the men had old ladies. Since it was family night and only old ladies were allowed with their kids, the single women stayed away. It wouldn't be until the old ladies left that the party went wild.

I wanted to be home before that even happened, but for now, I was enjoying myself talking with Tech, a club member who took care of the computer work, about gaming systems while eating a plate of food and drinking a soda.

"Lucas," Kylo bellowed from across the room with a big smile. I waved at him and returned his smile. It was the first time that night I'd seen him, but I'd heard he'd been busy outside helping his foster father with a bike. He'd taken him in after he got Kylo away from his parents.

"You know the prospect?" Tech asked as I watched Kylo approach.

"Yes, I met him at my brother's place about a month ago." Thinking of it reminded me we were getting close to having our parents back. They were arriving the following week, and I was looking forward to seeing them. "Do you know him?" I asked.

"Not really." I found that weird, so I looked at him. He winked before saying, "Not all the prospects make it through the long process to become a full member. I wait to see if they have what it takes."

"Fair enough." It was. I wouldn't want to become friends with someone who didn't stick around; then again, losing friends happened in everyday life.

"Prospect." Tech nodded when Kylo stopped in front of us.

"Tech, can I get you anythin'?" Kylo asked. Kylo had told me he was their lackey—anything they wanted he would have to get. Tech didn't seem too much older than Kylo and me, but he was a full member, so was to be respected by all prospects, which there were five of. Kylo was the only one I knew, but he'd said the other guys weren't too bad.

"Nah, I'm good. Sit and chat," Tech ordered.

"Thanks." Kylo grinned. "How're you enjoyin' family night?" Kylo asked me.

"It surprised me. I nearly pissed myself coming in, but it's been great. Met so many people and usually crowds and I don't get along. This here is more my standard. A small group to talk to, but I like watching others around me... and I think I'll shut up now, or I'll sound more like a creeper."

Both Tech and Kylo laughed. Zion and Death, who were standing close, also chuckled, obviously hearing me and my babble.

"I tend to over talk sometimes also," I explained to Tech.

"Wouldn't have guessed," he teased.

"Baby," a woman cried before she flung herself at Tech. Only Tech scowled at her in disgust. He grabbed her upper arms when she went to fling them around his neck.

"What the fuck?" he bit out low.

Death, Zion, and another biker surrounded Tech and the woman. Kylo took my plate and dropped it to the floor, then grabbed my wrist and pulled me to stand. He stepped us back a little.

"What's going on?" I whispered. Kylo just shook his head.

"Who let you in, Monday?" Tech asked, his voice darker than when he'd been speaking to me.

"Come on, honey. It's nearly time for the old ladies to leave, and I knew you'd want me in here."

"Your bitch ass was banned, Monday. You need to get the fuck out," Death said. All of them looked down at her in repulsion, with their upper lips raised.

"Oh, Tech didn't mean it when he told me not to come back."

"Whore, I did."

"What. The. Fuck!" got screeched.

"Shit," Zion clipped.

"Fuck." Death sighed.

"Eve, I've got this," Tech said to the woman who appeared out of nowhere. She looked similar to Tech; both had blond hair, caramel skin, and dark blue eyes.

"You got this? Is that why the bitch is on your lap?" She marched forward, grabbed the back of Monday's hair, and forced her from Tech's lap. Monday screamed out in pain and tried to slap at Eve's hand. Eve easily pulled her up and snarled in her face, "You think you can play my brother and come back in here like nothing happened? You need to get your dirty, rotting pussy out of here or I'll beat you so bad no man will want you."

"Eve," Death warned.

"Don't you Eve me, Death. It's family day, and she thinks—"

"The bitch is dead to us. You take her outside and make sure she gets the message, or we'll be delivering it ourselves."

Eve smiled a little crazy. "With pleasure." Still holding Monday's hair, Eve dragged her along, and people got out of the way. A few other women followed Eve out. There were others who laughed, some smiled, but none looked upset from the situation.

"You good, bro?" Zion asked.

"Um… yeah?"

The men around me laughed. Tech stood, slapped my back, and explained, "Don't worry, Lucas. The bitch has it coming. She cheated on me with a guy from another club. A club we're at war with. She knew if she did it, she would be out on her ass. Also, my sister's kind of protective."

Kind of.

"Ah, sorry she did that. Bitch is right." I blushed from using the cuss word.

More laughter surrounded me.

"Need a drink yet?" Kylo asked with a smirk.

"Ha! No, not yet." Since I wanted to be coherent tomorrow for more studying. "Though, if a full-on fight breaks out, I'll rethink it."

"Got it." He grinned. He said something else, but my attention snagged on something over near the bar. Since I was standing, I could see more of the room. Not much because I was short, but what I saw had my stomach churning.

Wreck stood at the bar, smiling down at a woman. A woman who had her hand resting on Wreck's arm. She flicked her hair over her shoulder and said something that had him laughing. I hadn't seen him laughing, and it was an amazing sight to see. However, it wasn't me who caused it.

It was a woman.

A *woman*.

He liked women.

Through everything, it was something I had forgotten.

"Hey, you all right?" Kylo asked.

"Huh? Oh, ah, yeah, yes. I'm good."

The woman ran her hand up Wreck's arm and cupped his cheek. He grinned down at her.

"Lucas?"

I blinked hard and ignored the twinge in my chest. "Sorry?" I asked Kylo as I looked back at him.

He shifted closer. "It was Wreck that West mentioned."

I snorted, fake laughed, and shook my head. "What? No, that's crazy."

"Sure it is. That's why you look sick with Sara being all over him."

I waved a hand in front of me. "I don't know what you're talking about. Is Wreck here?"

"You know he's not gay or bi, right?"

"Kylo, what are you talking about?"

"Don't lie to me. I thought we were friends. Why aren't you tellin' me the truth?"

I ground my teeth together and scrubbed a hand over my face. Leaning in, I whispered, "You can't say anything. Especially not to Wreck, but yes, I find him attractive."

Kylo groaned. "Lucas, that attraction will get you nowhere. He ain't like us."

I knew he wasn't, but why did he kiss me? I couldn't exactly say that, so I nodded. "I know. I'll get over it." I would because what I just saw would be burned in my mind as a reminder of why my heart would be crushed in the end. He loved women, not men. "I think I'll head home. Zion gave me the keys to the car since his ride was here. I'll talk to you soon, okay?"

Kylo patted my arm like he felt sorry for me. "Yeah, man. Drive safe."

I quickly said goodbye to those around us and made my way toward the door.

I will not look over there. I will not look over there. Dang it. I looked over there and found Wreck's eyes following me just as the woman, Sara, lifted up to press her lips against his.

CHAPTER ELEVEN
WRECK

*J*esus motherfucking hell. Why did this have to happen to me? I'd fucked up once more and wanted to bash myself in the face or have my brothers do it.

Not only did I lose my shit when Lucas went out on a goddamn date, and I was ready to tell him he was mine, that he couldn't see anyone else, but now he'd just seen Sara kiss me. His hurt was obvious in his eyes, even from all the way over the other side of the room. He probably thought I was just fucking with him and enjoyed sending him mixed signals. I wasn't, and I didn't.

Though, it kind of pleased me to see he was jealous. Then he'd know how I'd felt when he went out with that pissant. Only Lucas didn't know I'd claimed him. He didn't know I wanted him. He didn't know he was mine, but only because I hadn't said shit. I wanted to, yet there I was standing still and not chasing him because I was weak. I wanted to protect him. At least, that was what I thought I was doing, but really all I was doing was protecting myself from the judgment.

I had to man the fuck up, or he'd slip through my fingers.

"Christ," I clipped.

"What's wrong?" Sara asked. She was the daughter of a club

brother. If that wasn't reason enough to not touch her, there was also the fact she didn't do shit for me.

"Nothin', I gotta go." Where I didn't know. Everything in me wanted to rush after Lucas. Could I? Shit, I didn't fucking know. Though, what I did know, was that I didn't want Lucas with anyone.

No one was to touch him, or I'd lose my shit.

"Where are you going? I could come with you." She smiled seductively.

"Babe, you're a brother's daughter. It ain't happenin'."

She rolled her eyes. "I'm not wanting to become an old lady, Wreck. Just one night."

"And have Danger kill me? No thanks. Later," I told her before walking off. I'd meant to head to my room in the compound but found myself standing outside in the cool night air.

I ran a hand through my hair and then over my face.

"Fuck," I bit out.

If I didn't fix this, if I didn't tell Lucas he was mine, then there went my chance with him, and he'd probably end up in the arms of the fuckhead. Hell, if I even had a chance. Why did I want a chance? Because I couldn't stop thinking about him.

Shaking my head, I made my way to my car when someone stepped into my path.

"Where you goin'?"

Fuck.

Death stepped closer. He lifted a smoke and took a drag. The scent of pot wafted my way. "Just headin' out for a minute."

"Really? Why?"

"Gotta check the business out."

"We got brothers there already. You wanna tell me a new lie?"

I narrowed my gaze, crossed my arms over my chest, and demanded, "You wanna tell me where you *think* I'm goin'?" Death rarely got on my nerves, but he was starting to.

"Goin' to see Saint's brother."

Fucking shit.

I forced a laugh. "What the fuck you talkin' about?"

He chuckled. "Brother, don't bullshit a bullshitter. I ain't blind, and I'm sure Saint's cottoned on, but he won't say shit until he sees it with his eyes."

"What are you talkin' about?"

Death grinned, his white teeth flashing before he took another drag. He blew it out and said, "Know you, brother. Seen you watchin' him. Seen him watchin' you too, but you been fightin' within yourself. But it looks like you're done fightin'. Are you?"

Fuck it all. For Lucas. "Yes," I hissed.

His smile widened. "Good. But tread carefully. But I know you will 'cause it took you a month to finally fuckin' make up your mind."

"You done talkin?"

"Yep. I'll let you know when Saint leaves. Good luck," he finished, and then walked off whistling.

What the fuck just happened?

Death, my brother, gave me permission—not that I needed it—to pursue Lucas. Yeah, he said he saw us looking at each other, but how in the fuck did he get me wanting Lucas from that? More important, he was going to look out for me with Saint. I wasn't sure Saint would go for me being with his brother. Shit, I was really thinking of being with Lucas.

Well, dumb shit, you were seconds away from claiming him so no one else could have him, what do you think it means?

Yeah, all right, I was going to make Lucas mine.

At least I'd do everything in my power to make it happen. It could already be too late. I could have fucked everything up before it even started.

Shit, I was going to have to do some groveling. I'd never wanted to do it for anyone else. I'd fought with women before, knew it was my fault, yet had never found it in me to care enough about the woman to fight for her.

For Lucas, I would.

How fucking strange.

I stood in front of Saint and Lucas's place and checked the door. Lucas was lucky it was locked. I slipped out my keys and used the spare key I had for Saint's place, from the countless nights of crashing there, which hadn't happened in a while. My heart hammered in my chest, and my gut ate at my insides while my dick thickened slightly, as if it knew we were getting close to Lucas.

Opening the door, I stepped inside. The kitchen light was on, and I saw Lucas leaning against the counter, spooning ice cream from the tub into his mouth. He looked upset; there was no smile making him light up. He was slouched over the container like eating it could comfort him.

I did that to him.

I was sure of it and knowing it cut into me. I was surprised no blood showed.

His gaze didn't even lift when I'd opened and closed the door. He was in his own world again. It drove me crazy when he did this, but Jesus, he looked good.

His wild curls were everywhere. His plump lips, which I wanted to bite down on, were redder than normal from the cold ice cream. He wore a simple thin white tee with sweatpants, and still, my cock throbbed at the sight of his smaller but well-formed frame.

Moving closer, I saw Lucas suddenly lift his head, spot me, and freeze.

"Wreck," he whispered. He straightened and put the ice-cream tub on the counter behind him with the spoon in it. "Um, is Zion okay?"

I nodded.

His eyes ran over me quickly and then went back to my feet as he watched me walk even closer. It wasn't until I was in front of him that he pulled his eyes back up.

"What are you doing here?" His voice was soft, like a damn caress.

"She wasn't mine," I stated.

His brows creased. "Huh?" he asked, confused, and I wanted to kiss between his brows. Fuck, he was cute. Why did this attraction, this connection, even when there was more to know about the guy, happen with Lucas Storey?

"That woman at the compound I was talkin' to, she wasn't mine."

His chest rose and fell faster. I could see the pulse beating harder in his neck. He tilted his head to the side. "You came here to tell me that?"

"Yes."

"Why?"

Why… that was the question, and it was damn time to be honest.

"Because I want you to know. Because I can't fuckin' stop thinkin' about you." At least it was some of the truth. If I'd told him he was mine, and no one else could touch him, I worried it would freak him out. Already his eyes were wide, his breathing harder than before.

"Why?" he whispered.

I ignored it and asked my own question, "Did you kiss him? Did he touch you?"

He nodded, and I clenched my jaw to keep from cursing. I stepped closer. "Do you want him?" If he said yes, I was going to walk out of the house… or I was going to try.

He didn't answer, all he did was stare at my chest. God, he was short, the top of his head only reached my collarbone. But I still found him fucking perfect. A guy. A damn *guy*. I still couldn't figure out why or how he'd made me want him, how my body reacted to him, but it did, and all I wanted to do was curl him in my arms and protect him. There was also the need to be buried deep inside of his body.

Fuck, my cock jerked behind my jeans.

"Lucas, do you want him? If you say yes, I'll walk out right now."

He blew out a breath, shifted from one foot to another, and then planted both on the floor while he reached behind him to rest his hands on the counter. It looked like he was trying to hold himself up. Fucking cute. He cleared his throat. "And, um, let's just say, for testing purposes, that, ah, I was to say no… what would that mean?"

Reaching out, I gently pinched his chin and brought his gaze up to meet mine. "It'd mean I'd stay, and it'd mean me takin' your mouth like I want to."

He whimpered.

"Is that you sayin' you don't want him?"

He licked his lips and tipped his head up and down once.

"Fuck yes," I growled.

I slid my hand to the side of his neck and the other to his waist. I waited a beat to see if he'd back down. He didn't. He just kept looking at me with those damn sexy eyes.

"Last chance," I told him.

"F-For what?" he uttered.

"To tell me to fuck off because once I take your mouth again, once I taste what I've been cravin', then we're gonna see where this goes. Means you won't go out with anyone else. You get me?"

Lucas nodded, but I wasn't sure he completely understood. He'd learn with time. "Okay…," he muttered.

"You're sure?"

"Um, yes," he said softly, and when his eyes moved down to my mouth, I knew I wouldn't be able to walk away. Leaning in, I pressed my lips against his, once, twice, and on the third, I gripped him tighter and licked across his bottom lip. He gasped. I ate the sound down and glided my tongue inside.

Christ. Just as good as the first time. Only better.

I felt his hesitant hands touch my waist. He started to slide down like his legs weren't working, so I picked him up. He let out a yelp, and I sat his ass on the counter. I was so fucking pleased when he grabbed at me. He flung his arms around my neck, pulled me in, and he took my lips in a hard and hot kiss. Of course, I reciprocated, then took back control by reaching around, taking hold of the top of his ass, and dragging him forward. His legs opened and cradled my hips.

"Fuck," I clipped against his jaw. Both of us breathed hard. I wanted more yet though. I kissed my way to his neck, which he arched for me, and there I sucked on his skin, marking him for myself.

"Wreck," he whimpered.

Kissing where I'd been, I shook my head. "Wade. Call me Wade." I took his lips in another kiss and ran my hands up his back while his fingers ran up, gliding back and forth over the back of my head, feeling the rough buzz cut there.

He was driving me crazy. I expected to be freaked out since I didn't feel the press of breasts against my chest, but I wasn't. If anything, it was new and fucking exciting. My cock was rock hard. I tugged his lower body forward more and ground my cock into his. Another thing that didn't scare me, feeling how hard his dick was against mine. I liked knowing he was turned on as much as I was.

He pulled back panting. His warm eyes were wild. "Wade" was all he said.

"Bedroom?" I asked.

He nodded. But he bit his bottom lip, and it had me thinking he was worried.

I kissed him quickly, and said, "I ain't looking for more than you're willin' to give, Lucas. No pressure."

He let go of a heavy breath. "I… this… it's a little confusing still. You're here. You kissed me." He leaned in and lowered his voice. "You want to go to my room. With me. A guy."

I dropped a chuckle. "It's different for me, but as soon as I saw you, I couldn't keep my eyes off you. You're fuckin' stunnin'.'"

His cheeks coated in red and he dropped forward, burying his head in my shoulder. Did he know how sexy he was? Had no one complimented him on it before? Shit, he would have noticed men and women checking him out. I saw it with my own damn eyes at the compound. Brothers who probably weren't even into guys were looking at him appreciatively. The women were the worst though. They eyed him like they wanted to lift their skirt and have him fuck them right there and then. It'd surprised the fuck out of me because most were old ladies to hardass bikers, yet they saw Lucas—cute, timid, but sexy-as-fuck Lucas—and would have done anything for him if he'd asked.

"You'd get many dicks hard, Lucas."

"Stop it," he mumbled against me.

Smiling, all I could think was how goddamn cute he was.

"All right, I'll stop for now." Hell, I couldn't stop grinning. His shyness, his innocence, was a turn-on. I had him in my arms. I had *Lucas Storey* in my arms. I'd been kissing him. Now there was no way I would give him up for anything or anyone.

We'd take it slow, get him used to it, to me, and get others used to the idea of me being with a man. There'd be times where I wouldn't be sure of myself, but fucking hell, I was sure about the man against my chest.

Stepping back, I helped Lucas to his feet. He swayed forward a little, and I steadied him.

"That was your fault," he said.

Chuckling, I replied, "Fair enough." Jesus, I hadn't felt this light in a damn long time. He caused this, made me feel like a fucking teen knowing I was going to get me some. Even if it was making out for the rest of the night, I would be happy with that.

What the fuck?

Me. I would be happy just kissing?

That was when I realized I had it bad.

I couldn't ruin this.

CHAPTER TWELVE
LUCAS

If Wreck—Wade—wasn't holding my hand, he would see how much it shook like the other one. I was a mess, body and mind. I didn't know if I should be pushing him away and telling him to get out or rejoicing because he kissed me stupid, and then maybe I could offer myself up on a platter. Naked.

Kicking him out would probably be the safest.

So why was I following him down the hall to my bedroom?

Maybe it was because he'd left the compound, the party, to come after me and set me straight. Maybe it was because he found me attractive and told me he couldn't get me off his mind. Those two things I still couldn't get over. Shock kept me walking. He'd chased *me*. He'd said *I* was attractive when he'd had a beautiful woman in front of him. He'd wanted me. *Me*!

I mean, the kiss we'd shared weeks ago was out-of-my-mind hot, but then he'd sent me that text. I'd thought he'd had his fun, and that was done. Obviously not, because what we'd just done in the kitchen blew even the first kiss out of the water.

Wade glanced back with a small smile that shot me straight to the groin. It wasn't only my stomach in knots from excitement and nerves; it felt like my whole body was. Only my dick was ready for something to happen. It had started to get hard when I first saw Wade, then grown with what he said and the kissing. Now I was already leaking in my boxers. I wanted to look down to see if it was visible, but knowing my luck, Wade would glance back in that exact moment, and I wouldn't be able to look at him for the rest of the time. And I wanted to look at him. I had to make sure he was still there, real, and wanting me.

He wanted me.

Wreck— Wade… whatever his last name was. I really had to find that out.

We entered my room. Wade shifted me to the side of the door with his hands on my waist, then closed the door, all while watching me, causing my stomach to dip.

"At your pace, Lucas," he said again.

I nodded, and a curl dropped into my eyes. Before I could brush it away, Wade was there, taking it between a finger and thumb. He gave it a tug, staring at it as it straightened and then watched how it sprang back up once he let go. He then brushed it behind my ear and traced the outer shell of my ear. I shivered, lost in the feeling, and witnessing him be so gentle.

"Fuckin' love your hair."

"Really?" I blurted before I could stop myself.

"Really," he said as he threaded his fingers through my hair and gripped tightly, causing me to gasp. His eyes intensified, burning into me. Gently, he pushed me back, so I touched the wall. He stepped in and slowly lowered his head.

"Fuckin' love these lips," he said against said lips before taking my mouth in a fierce kiss. I lifted my shaking hands and pushed his vest from his shoulders. When it was down to his elbows, I paused at my bold move. Wade lifted his head. I knew I was blushing brightly. I didn't want him to think I wanted everything that night. I wasn't ready for everything. But I also wanted him comfortable, wanted him on my bed to make out a bit more, and maybe reach second base. Light groping to a point we both released our loads sounded good to me, and I was happy to do that with our clothes on. Since his body was fit and mine was… well, mine, smaller in every way than what Wade was, I just knew—from living with Zion—that they were particular with their vests. They treated them with care, placed them down, didn't throw or put them anywhere in jeopardy.

But how did I tell him all that?

It felt like I was still learning words when he was around. Especially when he drove me as crazy as he was with his eyes and hands still gripping me.

"Um," I started and then licked my lips, to which he growled low at. Oh boy, that was hot. It made me think he wanted to be the one to lick my lips. He'd already done it, but it felt as if he wanted to be the only one to do it, that I had no right to my lips, only him.

"I, ah… you see… you, me, clothes on, but fool around. Except vest?"

His smile was the biggest I'd ever seen on him. He chuckled, seeming satisfied. "So fuckin' cute," he muttered before giving me a peck and stepping back to remove his vest before laying it carefully over the back of my swivel chair. He kicked off his boots, then took off his socks and lifted his chin toward the bed. "Get on," he ordered.

Thankfully, I was twenty-two and not some thirteen-year-old just learning what it felt like coming and wanting to do it every second of the day because I would have come in my boxers right there and then.

But I discovered I liked being told what to do. Especially the way Wade did it.

My steps were faster than I should have shown in front of him, but I wanted to get there, get him back in my arms with his mouth on me in any way.

He gave off a light chuckle, and I knew he was thinking about me being cute. Usually I would take offense. I wasn't cute. I was sexy and hot, but I didn't mind the way Wade said it. It made me feel like in that one word, he actually meant all those things put together.

Climbing on the bed, I lay back on my pillow and looked at the man in front of me. He stood at the end of the bed, staring down at me with heat in his eyes. Heat for me. A guy.

How did I get so lucky?

I bit my bottom lip. I couldn't think about anything other than what was happening in the moment, or my mind would get carried away, and fear could settle in, causing me to clam up and push him away. I didn't want that.

"Fuckin' sexy," he told me.

Rolling my eyes, I shook my head. "You don't have to say—"

"Don't," he ordered on a growl. "If I didn't find you goddamn sexy, I wouldn't have this." He palmed his hard erection behind his jeans. My cock jerked behind my sweatpants, which was on more of a display since I was lying back. Wade shook his head. "I wouldn't be hard for you, Lucas. Hard because of your look, your voice, the things you do." He kneeled on the end of the bed, then bent, his hands to the covers as he slowly crawled up over me. He dipped, pressed his lips to mine once, twice. "You drive me insane."

"S-So do you." I blinked. "I mean, ah, that you drive me, um, insane."

Wade smirked. When his hand touched at my waist, I jolted, still not expecting his ease at touching me. His smirk grew into a smile, and he trailed his fingers up my side. I slapped a hand over my mouth when laughter burst out of me.

Wade's eyes met mine, one brow rose.

"Sorry," I mumbled. "I'm ticklish."

He grinned. "Good to know." He didn't stop his path, causing me to laugh again, but when his hand rested against the side of my throat, I sobered. His intense look had me breathing faster, had my pulse ticking wilder. "Open those legs for me," he ordered.

I did. He lowered his bottom half over me. I quickly bit my bottom lip to stop myself from moaning when his erection rubbed against mine. Instead, I whimpered and gripped the backs of his biceps to hold on.

"Christ," Wade hissed, and all I could do was nod. Did he feel as lost as I did? Lost in desire? Spreading my legs more, I pressed my feet into the bed and ground up into him. His jaw clenched, his eyes closed, and again he cursed, "Christ."

Yes, he was as lost as I was, and seeing it had me smiling, even at a time like that. I ground up again, and his eyes flashed open. He growled in the back of his throat, and then he was kissing me like he had no other choice.

I pushed all my worries away and just let myself live in the moment because I couldn't have tried to stop it if I wanted to. Wade was there in my room, in my arms, on my bed.

It was a fantasy come true.

The kiss grew urgent. We tasted, teased, and rubbed against one another. I touched him in every place I could—his back, his hair, his neck, his butt. Our movements became jerky, and my balls were singing their praises because I was so close to an end I knew I would enjoy.

I didn't even care about my embarrassment after the moment. I was going to ride this orgasmic roller coaster right to the end.

I tightened my thighs around Wade's hips and pushed myself up and down faster. I slid both hands up and under his tee, touching his warm skin, wishing I'd taken the time to investigate his naked chest before we'd started the dry humping.

Dear God, we were dry humping, and it felt wonderful.

No, amazing.

I mumbled incoherently against his delicious lips.

"Fuck, what?" he asked, kissing down my neck.

He bit. I moaned. "I… we… gonna come," I warned.

He groaned and bit again, then sucked on me where my neck and shoulder met, only he didn't stop moving. His hands slid under my ass, and he held me tightly while we moved against each other.

"Wade, so close," I warned again.

He grunted, trailed his lips back up to mine, and kissed me again.

It was then my body tensed for a second, my balls shot up inside me, and my load erupted into my pants. I whimpered, moaned, and called his name over and over.

"Fuck," he clipped and then grunted, still rocking into me. When he pressed his head into my shoulder and panted through breaths, I knew he'd also found the end in the moment.

I hugged him tightly to me, not wanting this moment to end. Gently, I traced my hands up and down his back. I knew we would part, things would get awkward, well, on my part, but right then, I didn't care. I wanted to hold Wade just a bit longer.

"Am I hurtin' you?" he asked softly.

"No," I told him and went back to caressing his skin.

"We need to talk."

I shook my head. "Not yet." I was close to falling asleep, and I could tell by the way Wade's body pressed into me, he was relaxing even more onto me.

Until he lifted off me, pressed a quick kiss to my lips, and said, "Be back." Then he was off the bed and walking from the room. The air cooled, his warmth gone, and I shivered from the chill. At first, I panicked he'd just up and left, but I heard him in the bathroom, and my heart was back to bouncing around in my body in nerves and excitement.

Wade was cleaning himself up.

Wade had come in his jeans.

I made Wade come.

Wade, who was Wreck, just came like a horny teen because we'd been kissing.

I hid my giggle behind my hands. Holy cannoli, that actually happened.

Glancing to the door when I heard him move back toward my

bedroom, I saw him walk in. His jeans were undone, and I could see he had nothing on under them. Then I noticed he held a wet washcloth. Smiling shyly, I held out my hand, "Thanks."

He smirked but didn't give it to me. Instead, he sat on the bed at my hip, and before I could stop him, he had the front of my pants and boxers down cleaning up the mess.

My face ignited. "Oh my God, I can do that." I tried to grab for it, but Wade pushed my hands away.

"I've got it."

I could see he had, but the problem with him staring at my cock and messing around near it, my dick thought it was time to play again and hardened.

He paused, met my gaze, and smirked.

"I can't help it," I blurted.

He chuckled. "Good to know." He dropped the washcloth to the floor and readjusted my pants. "You might wanna change. Your boxers are wet."

"Uh-huh" was all I could say.

He smiled. "Fuckin' cute. We gotta talk before I get."

Was he going? My stomach clenched. Was this a hit-and-dash moment?

"Hey," he called. "Fuck, come here," he said, but before I could move, he picked me up and set me on his lap.

Oh wow. He was strong.

"Jesus, you're small."

"I think you saw I wasn't small—"

He burst out laughing. He leaned down and kissed my neck. "I wasn't talkin' about your dick, Lucas. Just how short you are. So easy to move you around."

My face and neck burned with mortification. "Oh," I muttered.

He gripped my hair and tugged my head back so I would look at him. "Christ," he murmured before he kissed me again. Groaning, he pulled away. "You're addictive. But I gotta head off soon because I gotta be up early for my shift at the Polished Pussy."

"Um, okay."

He smiled. "Wishin' I could stay and lay with you."

My head jerked back in surprise. "You do?"

"Hell yes. What this is, what's started, isn't endin'. We just gotta take shit slow. It's new territory. I wanna know you before others can see what we got. Understand?"

I licked my lips. "I think so."

"It'll do, for now." Wade's hands moved to my waist. When his grip tightened, I gave him my attention again. "You got school tomorrow?"

"Yes."

"Are you workin' after?"

I shook my head. "Not until Thursday night."

"All right. I'll try and catch you tomorrow, but I'll have to see how things are at work and the club. Unless you don't wanna see me?"

"No, I want to," I said too quickly and witnessed Wade's smug smile.

"Good." His smile faded. "We get us sorted before others know, yeah?"

"Yes, Wade."

"No seein' that jackass."

I rolled my eyes. "We go to the same college, have a class together."

"Then you set him straight."

"About?"

He flared. "About you not wantin' to see him again."

"Um, okay, but it's fine as friends, right?"

Something crossed his face as he let out a breath. "As long as he doesn't touch you."

My eyes widened. A part of me liked his possessiveness, where a smaller part said it was too much. For now, I would let it rest. I wanted to please him. He wanted something more with me. He wanted me… but would he crush me after a week? A month? Would he realize I wasn't worth the trouble? When it came to it, would he really want people to know we were something?

My head ached from all the thoughts crossing my mind.

"Hey," Wade said. "Where'd you go?"

I shrugged. I couldn't tell him my fears. Insecurity was never attractive, which I knew I was, but I'd never had a relationship…. Could I even call this a relationship? Was Wade telling me we were dating? Was he my boyfriend?

"Lucas," Wade clipped low. "Whatever you're thinkin', stop. We'll take each day as it comes. You willin' to do that with me?"

Was I?

I wanted to try, but worry had me keeping my mouth closed.

"You're worried," he stated, reading my mind. "Talk to me, Lucas. We need to be straight with each other."

"You've only ever been with women?"

"Yeah," he said, almost hesitantly.

"I'm a guy."

He snorted. "Know that."

"Are *you* sure this is what you want?" I had to ask, or else I would worry for the rest of the night.

"Fuck yes. Want nothin' more in my life but this."

"Then why—"

"The text?" he asked and frowned.

I nodded.

"Because I'm a dickhead. Because you gave me the best goddamn kiss of my life and it scared me. I wanted to protect you because I was mixed up in the head. But, Lucas, I want to try this with you. I'm gonna fuck up, you might need patience, but I'll try my damn best."

Oh shit, oh shit, oh shit.

I wasn't going to tear up like some idiot, but what he'd just said warmed me throughout, and my emotions clung to him some more.

Dropping my head, I thumped it against his shoulder. "Okay," I whispered.

"Yeah?"

"Yes."

"Good, now kiss me before I leave," he ordered, and my dick jerked in my pants.

Since it was what I wanted as well, I did as I was told and kissed him, letting him know in the kiss how I knew I would miss him.

CHAPTER THIRTEEN
WRECK

I scrubbed a hand over my face as I walked into the compound. I couldn't wipe the smile off my face from thinking about Lucas. Even when I didn't get much sleep and had kept fighting with myself to go back to him. I couldn't, though, because Saint would be there.

Christ, I hadn't been this fucking happy in a long time. It wasn't that I was just happy, and this was going to sound pathetic, but it was as if a hole inside of me I hadn't known about had been filled by Lucas.

It'd killed me waiting last night to see if he wanted to give this a chance without telling anyone. I knew he'd have his doubts. I was a bastard to begin with, but there he was taking me up on my offer to see where this would go.

Shit.

Lucas was mine.

I grabbed my phone out, wanting to reach out to Lucas before I walked into a room full of brothers.

Me: When do you get home?
Lucas: Who is this?

Me: Me.

Lucas: Me who? Sorry, I don't have your number in my contacts.

Well, shit, he must have deleted it after I was a motherfucker.

Me: The man who made you come last night.

Lucas: OMG, Wade! I'm in a classroom full of people. You can't say stuff like that.

Me: Why? You don't like it?

Lucas: It's not that... I like it a little too much.

Me: You getting hard?

Lucas: Yes! Great, now my face is on fire and people are looking at me.

Me: I'm not laughing. Save my number. Promise I won't send shit texts again.

Lucas: Okay.

Hell, if he'd been around me saying that, I knew he would have said it in a whisper. Now my dick was stiffening, and it definitely wasn't the time.

Me: You didn't answer my question. When do you get home?

Lucas: Don't get grumpy.

I pulled my brows together. Now, why would he say that?

Me: Lucas.

Lucas: Wade, it's okay, I just have a study date after class I forgot about.

Me: Date as in date, date?

Jesus, I sounded like an idiot, but I needed clarification.

Lucas: NO. Not a date, date. We get together and study.

Me: Who. Will. Be. There?

Lucas: If you relax, I'll tell you.

Me: I am relaxed.

Lucas. Sure you are. Do you have a tight grip on your phone?

Fuck. Maybe I had, but he didn't need to know that.

Me: Lucas, tell me.

Lucas: Fine, West will be there, along with Lani and Gregory.

Me: Fuckface is going? Did you tell him?

Lucas: I haven't seen him to tell. I won't do it over the phone. I'll let him know.

Me: Where's this study date?

Lucas: Library, so it's out in the open WITH other people there.

Lucas: Wait. Don't you dare think of showing up.

Smiling, I didn't answer. It would be best not to lie at the start of the relationship.

Lucas: Wade! Answer me. Do not show up!

Lucas: Wade!

Me: Got to go, got church with the brothers.

Lucas: Wade, don't think I didn't notice you didn't say anything! On a side note: you go to church with the others???

Chuckling, I shook my head.

Me: Not church, Lucas. It's a meeting with all of us but it's called church.

Lucas: Oh. All right, have fun in church.

Me: Talk soon!

Lucas: Can I just say I like texting with you. I like talking with you and looking at you. I also like where this is going with us.

Christ, my heart gave a hard thump in my chest, and my gut was dancing around like a girl's. He made me feel, and it was fucking good.

Me: How's the blushing going now?

Lucas: It's bad.

Me: Wish I could see, and Lucas, I like all those things with you too.

Lucas: I'm glad, but you still can't come to the library. Promise, please.

Laughing, I shook my head.

Me: Later.

Lucas: Wade (whatever your last name is) I can handle this.

Me: It's Williams, and I know you can.

Lucas: I feel like you left off a but at the end. However, there shouldn't be a but.

There was one hell of a big but on the end, and it would be: but I was still going because even though I knew he could handle it, I still wanted to be there as backup, and I didn't want fuckface to even try to touch him.

Lucas: I'm sighing right now. Anyway, have a good church meeting. Don't reply to this text because then I'll want to reply because I like to be the last one to respond and I'll feel like I need to respond more if you write back to me. And I've rambled, but you'll have to get used to this. Plus, my teacher is now getting suspicious. Bye!

Goddamn, he was cute.

Still grinning, I walked into the room church was held in to find everyone was already there.

"Look here, brothers, Wreck's smilin'. Do we need to worry?" State, our vice president, taunted.

"Fuckin' A we need to worry. Can't remember the last time I've seen it," Country, our president, added.

Saint joined in with "Someone got himself some."

If he only fuckin' knew who it was with. Then again, I wanted to live longer so I was glad he didn't.

I scowled. "Shut the fuck up," I snarled.

The brothers laughed, but it was Death who said, "There he is. For a moment, I worried you were a Stepford wife."

Asshole, he knew exactly who I was smiling about.

"Can we get this meetin' started?" I asked, taking a seat at the long oval table next to Death.

"You got somewhere to run off to?" State asked with a smirk. I shot him the middle finger. He laughed and then nodded to Country.

Country lifted the gavel and smacked it down. "Shut the fuck up, everyone, church is startin'." He took a breath and leaned forward. "Brothers, can't fuckin' say enough about how proud I am of our club. The new charter is runnin' smoothly so far. Our businesses—Polished Pussy, Meat 'n' Eat, Fitness For You, and We Got You, Protection Agency—are boomin'. Shit is lookin' good. We need to keep this shit up, but I'm not damn stupid. I know things can't be good forever. We need to stay vigilant. Quake, anythin' we need to know about those motherfuckers?" Country meant our rival club that wanted to deal their coke in our territory. We didn't deal in drugs or guns. Yeah, we smoked some pot, we had guns to protect ourselves, but we wouldn't sell any of that shit. Country wanted our family protected from that crap, and he made sure of it. In whatever way we could. Sometimes it was ways that were illegal, but we got stuff done and made sure to anyone else watching, it was clean. Made sure the cops stayed off our backs. Especially since there were some detectives who had a hard-on for Country and wanted to end our club in any way they could.

It wouldn't happen though. We wouldn't allow it.

We may deal in pussy, but even that was clean. It was a legal business where we were located in Nevada. Hell, there were other brothels around, but since we opened and we had women who were stunning, we'd been run off our feet. Men traveled from all over the world to get themselves some. I co-owned it along with Saint, State, and Country. Death owned and ran the security business, and Quake owned five butcher shops around. All brothers helped out and worked within the club or businesses. We ran a tight ship, and it was looking great for us.

Country nodded after Quake finished going over things. "Thanks, Quake. We'll be sure to keep our eyes open. Right, movin' on. Saint, you said you had an idea for Polished Pussy," Country said.

"I do. Been thinkin' of addin' guys to the list instead of just women. My bro made a point that not only are guys interested in gettin' themselves some, but it could be good for the married women. Some husbands would even pay to watch their women with men."

Country shared a look with State, then said, "Sounds good, but we'd have to make sure whoever we hired is willin' to swing both ways."

"Sure, we could find some bi guys as well as gay ones."

Someone laughed. "You could get your brother to test out the gay ones."

A hand dropped to my arm. I realized I'd been ready to jump across the table to strangle Hemp for that suggestion. Luckily, Death caught my attention with his hard grip.

"You can fuck right off, Hemp. You say anythin' about my brother, I'll kill you," Saint warned.

"I'll back you up. The kid's a good one," Tech added.

"I'm positive Wreck and I'll help as well," Death said.

I would be the first to take the fucker down if he said more about Lucas. Suddenly, I didn't give a fuck if he knew I wanted to be with Lucas. I'd rather take all the shit, so Lucas didn't have to deal with any of it. When the time came for it to be out, I'd make sure that happened. Lucas didn't need any crap from anyone. Especially a brother.

Hemp's hands came up. "Sorry, brothers, just messin'. Didn't actually mean it. I wouldn't even say shit to your bro, Saint. Met him last night and know he's a good kid."

"He is," Saint grumbled. "And if any of you dickheads have anythin' to say about him being gay, I won't stand for it, let that be known."

"Relax, brother," Country said. "No one will say anythin'. We ain't bigots here. Each to their own and whatever makes them happy for fuck's sake. If anyone does have a problem, they keep it to themselves. Yeah, brothers?"

There was a chorus of agreements, and it settled my anger a little. I still wanted to smack Hemp around though.

Once the meeting came to an end, I walked out and knew Death followed me. Knew he was going to say something, so I made my way to my room. I entered with Death still on my tail.

Turning, I watched him shut the door and lean against it. He was smiling. I rolled my eyes and crossed my arms over my chest.

"Guess you and Lucas worked things out."

I pulled up my brows. "What makes you say that?"

"The smile when you walked in, the rip-you-apart look you shared with Hemp." He shrugged. "Easy to pick up, really."

"Only because you knew where I was goin'."

"That's true. You gonna tell me what the go is?"

I hesitated, unsure if Lucas would want me to say anything. Hell, we were only starting out. "Just gonna see how things go."

"But you like him?"

"Jesus fuckin' Christ, are you seriously askin' this?"

"Yep."

"I'll quote Lucas, my personal life ain't any of your business. Or anyone's."

He snorted. "Fair. But you sure this is what you want? I mean, really think about this, Wreck. I can see Lucas makes you happy I can see you like the guy, but think outside your box. You were into women before him. Will this last? Will Saint be all right with it? I don't want to see either of you hurt, brother."

I ground my teeth together. He wouldn't understand. I'd fought with myself for a fucking month and got nowhere but an ache in my head and chest. I couldn't step back now, not when I had him. I couldn't give Lucas up. Was that being selfish? Maybe, but I could tell from his looks, his touches, he wanted me and wanted to try this between us as much as I wanted it.

"I want this. Lucas wants this. We're goin' to see where its goin', no matter what anyone says. The fuckin' first time I saw him he appealed to me like no one else had. I can't make sense of it, but it is what it is. I won't fuckin' fight this anymore."

His smile grew, then he laughed. "Congrats, brother, and good luck."

I took a deep breath to calm myself. "Thanks." I nodded. I removed my vest and tee, then pulled out a warmer shirt.

"Whoa, brother, I know you're into guys now, but I ain't there."

Snorting, I told him, "Fuck off. Gotta head out."

"Goin' to see your man?" Death teased.

He was being a dick, but I wouldn't say no to Lucas being mine. "He's got a study date with a few people."

"One of them that guy he went out with?"

"Yes," I hissed.

Death chuckled. "Want any help?"

"It'll be fine."

"Can I just come for entertainment purposes?"

Fuck it. "Sure."

"I'll go grab a jacket and meet you out front."

"Death?"

"Yeah, brother?"

"Thanks for acceptin' this, for havin' my back."

"Always, brother. Can't help who you like. Hell, I can see the appeal. Lucas is damn good-lookin'." His hands shot up when I scowled at him. "But, brother, he ain't my type."

I paused from pulling on my vest. "You got a type? Are you into guys?"

Death shook his head. "Nah, brother, but I'm one who can admit there are men out there that are damn good-lookin'. Not as good as me, of course."

I scoffed. "You sure your head will fit out the fuckin' door?"

He opened it, stepped out, and grinned like a fucking fool. "Well, see that." He winked. "See you out front."

"Got it." Only then I realized that Lucas didn't know that Death knew. I wasn't sure how Lucas would take it. All I could imagine was him bumbling over his words while blushing and maybe growling in the back of his throat when he got frustrated. Smiling to myself, I knew no matter, I couldn't wait to see him.

Looked like what I'd told him would be out the window soon. I'd told him I wanted to keep it between us while we got to know one another, yet Death knew, soon West would, and fuckface. At least with Death there, we'd be able to scare the others shitless to keep their mouths shut before Saint got between us with his threats. I wanted us to be stronger before that happened because I didn't want to worry that Lucas would listen to his brother.

CHAPTER FOURTEEN
LUCAS

"Why do you keep looking over at the door?" West asked while we waited for the rest of the group.

Because my, ah, boyfriend was going to show and probably make Gregory pee himself. I wanted to speak with Gregory as soon as he showed before Wade arrived. I just prayed Gregory would get there first.

"Um, no reason. Just waiting on the others," I told West. A hand stopped me bouncing my pen up and down on the table. I looked down and then up to West.

"You're nervous. Why? Is it because of Gregory? I thought the date went well. Unless… are you excited to see him?"

I laughed nervously. "I wouldn't say excited. I think I might throw up."

"Did he do something?"

"No! He was fine. It's all fine, and we will be fine."

"That's a lot of fine. Lucas, you're scaring me. What's going on? And why are you wearing a turtleneck in here? It doesn't get that cold."

Right, why was I wearing one? Because my boyfriend—there was that giddy feeling in my stomach at that word—left his mark on my body, and I had to hide it. Which made me all types of buttery on the inside because he felt he had to leave me marked.

"I just thought, since it's cold outside, it might be in here."

West looked at me like I was an alien. "How many times have you been here in the winter and it's not freezing enough for a turtleneck?"

"Well—"

"Hey, sorry I'm late. Lani can't make it either," Gregory announced, and I yelped at the sudden new voice to the table. Then when he dipped down as if to kiss me, I pulled back so fast my chair tipped, and I fell on the floor.

"Ow," I moaned.

"Shit, are you okay?" Gregory asked.

West was too busy laughing to get up and help me. Gregory held his hand out toward me, but I didn't take it. I got to my feet slowly, knowing I probably resembled a lobster.

"Sorry about that," I offered Gregory.

"Have I done something?" he asked, reaching out to take my hand. I went to pull it back, but I felt terribly guilty for my actions already. It wasn't Gregory's fault. I was the one being an ass and dating Wade instead of him. Especially when I'd kissed Gregory a week ago, and we'd shared a small peck on campus about four days ago. He'd even had his arm around my seat in class like we had been dating.

My stomach twisted in an ugly way for the way I was.

"No, it's all my fault. I'm so sorry," I said, taking his hand. I glanced at West. "Can you give us a moment, please?"

He was busy holding his belly from the laughing he was still doing. He nodded, got up, and walked off into an aisle.

Gregory and I sat. Gregory took my hand again, and I glanced at the doors. I didn't know what time Wade would show, but what I did know was that Wade would definitely show.

"Um, look, I, ah, there's no easy way saying this, but I think I've led you to believe we're something more than what I saw it as, and

I'm so sorry about it. I didn't mean to. I would hate to hurt anyone's feelings."

Oh, dear God, he looked like he was about to cry.

"Lucas," West said behind me.

I squeezed Gregory's hand and looked down at the table because I didn't want to see the hurt on his face anymore. "Gregory, please forgive me, but I can't. We won't…. I'm not looking at dating anyone right now…." A throat cleared. "Actually, that's not true, and I want to be honest with you. I am seeing someone. It was unexpected, but… um, you see, I… he was an ass just before we went out, and then he redeemed himself and now… well, I'm kind of stuck on him."

"Lucas," West hissed. He even pinched my side.

I glanced up and over my shoulder, glaring at West. His head tipped to the side a couple of times. I shifted around in my seat to look and froze.

Dang it all.

Wade *and* Death stood there. One glared, and the other grinned down at me.

I wheezed a little, then coughed, and finally asked, "How much did you hear?"

"I think we arrived at the table just in time to hear all of it." Death smirked.

"You want to release him now?" Wade growled.

My hand was dropped like it was on fire, and I looked back at Gregory to see him staring up at Wade and Death like they were soul suckers coming to take him to hell.

"Ah, hi!" I said cheerily. "How are you both? West, do you remember Wade, I mean Wreck and Death? You remember them, right?" I nudged West in the leg with my elbow.

"Sure," West drew out. "Except I haven't met Death before."

Death's hand came out, and West shook it. "Nice to meet ya." Death nodded.

"Likewise. But can I ask why you two are in the college library?"

He paused, and I could feel him look from Wade to me, to Wade and back again. "Hang on, are you and—"

"Lucas," Wade said, still in a growly tone, and if I didn't lock my body down, I would have shivered because it reminded me of the noises he'd made while coming.

"Uh, Lucas, you're burning up there," West said before laughing quietly.

"Right, um…" I stood. "Anyway, it was great to see you both, but we're just going to study." I nodded and rested my hands against Wade's chest to push him back. He didn't move.

Instead, he took hold of my arm and moved me to the side where Death spun me to stand behind him. I peeked around to see Death was no longer smiling.

Wade leaned forward, resting his fists onto the table. "You understand what Lucas said?"

Gregory nodded.

"Wade," I snapped low.

"Good. He didn't mean to lead you on. I fucked up with him, but now I know I want him, and he wants me. What you gotta understand is I don't like anyone to fuck with what's mine. I don't like anyone to touch what's mine. Lucas is mine."

"Holy shit, this is awesome," West said.

"All right." Gregory nodded.

"Wade," I bit out.

"Shh," West said to me.

Wade leaned in more, and Gregory whimpered in fear. "Saw you outside before." Gregory's eyes widened. "Call him here." Gregory gulped. "Now," Wade ordered.

"What's going on?" I demanded.

When Gregory didn't move, Wade hit the table. We got a lot more attention from people around us then. I looked over to the counter and thanked God the librarian wasn't there, or she would have been over quickly shushing us and then kicking us out.

"Look away," Death warned, and people went back to whatever they were doing.

It was magic, or they were scared. Probably the latter because if I didn't know them, I would be as well.

"Call," Wade said again, and Gregory took out his phone, pressed something in, and put it to his ear.

I moved from behind Death to Wade's back and touched him. "Wade, what's going on?" I whispered.

"Just wait, Lucas, please," he asked, still staring down at Gregory.

West shifted closer to me, and out of the corner of his mouth, he asked, "This is epic. I didn't hear things, right? You and him?"

I nodded. West smiled widely.

"H-Hi, can you come inside the library so we can talk? N-No, he's not here. Okay."

When Gregory hit the End button, Wade said, "Death, over by the door and make sure he comes over to the table."

"On it, brother." Death walked over near the door and stood just inside it with his arms crossed and a cranky look on his face.

Wade then ordered, "You move, I'll fuckin' end you."

Gregory nodded. He glanced at me and pleaded, "Lucas, I didn't mean to do this, but I had to. I had to because he has something on me, said he would show it publicly, and if my dad finds out, I'll be dead. Please, I didn't mean this."

"What is this?" I asked.

Wade straightened. He turned to me and cupped the side of my face. "You know I have your back, yeah?" I nodded. "I'll always protect you because you're mine."

"Okay," I whispered.

"Lucky bastard," West muttered.

"Good, now kiss me and just watch. Don't say anythin'. I'll take care of it."

"Okay." I nodded, lost in his words, in his warm eyes that were just for me.

"Lucas," Wade said with a smile.

"Hmm?"

"Fuckin' kiss me," he demanded.

Lifting to my toes, I pressed my lips to his. I heard gasps and murmurs but ignored them all. I didn't care who saw that Wade was into me. He was mine, and like he'd said, I was his.

Except then I remembered Death was in there. I pulled back and looked over my shoulder to find Death grinning at us.

"He knows. He'll keep it quiet until we tell Saint."

"Oh, um, okay… he's okay with it?"

Wade chuckled. "Yeah. Now go sit down around the other side of the table." He turned to West. "Go sit with him."

"Yes, captain." West saluted and guided me around the table with a hand to my lower back.

"Know you two are friends, but keep the touchin' to nothin', yeah?" Wade said.

West grinned and gave him both thumbs-up. "You got it." We both sat down and waited for this mystery person to arrive. I didn't know what was going on, but I knew Wade didn't like what he'd obviously heard, so he was fixing it.

My heart felt like it had taken over my whole body with how much giddiness I was feeling.

I admired Wade as he stood in front of Gregory, facing the door with his legs spread a little, and his arms crossed over his chest. God, he looked good.

My mind still hadn't settled on the fact he and I were dating. I'd found it easier just to call him my boyfriend, but to know we were dating, courting, in a relationship. Yes, my brain was still taking time to process.

I could have second-guessed what we'd had, but in front of West and Death, he'd claimed me as his to Gregory, and they'd heard. Heck, he'd even wanted a kiss in front of everyone. He didn't shy away from public displays of affection. That still had me grinning like a maniac. All I wanted to do was jump him, but I didn't think the library was the right place to do that. A kiss was okay in front of people, but screwing wasn't, unfortunately.

"I want to know all about this later," West whispered.

"Maybe," I teased. I would let him know the minor details, but not all of it. That was just for Wade and me.

I glanced at Gregory, and he looked green. I was back to feeling guilty. I should have waited before I started anything with him, but then again, I never expected Wade to come to me asking for a second chance.

West knocked his knee against mine and nodded to the door. We both turned that way. My eyes widened when Mitch Henry, my nemesis, walked in. He took one look at me, then Wade, and turned back around, but Death was there waiting.

"Get the fuck over there," Death ordered.

"Stop it. What is this?" Mitch asked, his voice high in worry. He tried to push back at Death, but Death didn't move. When they were close, Wade grabbed the back of Mitch's shirt, twisted him, and sat him in the chair next to Gregory. Death stood behind him and placed a hand on Mitch's shoulder. When he went to get up, Death pushed him back down.

Wade took the seat next to Mitch and stared down at him while Mitch waved his hands around. "I don't understand any of this." He glared across at me. "This is your fault. I just know it. I'm going to make sure you suffer."

"Stop," Wade snarled. "Shut the fuck up," he added.

"I didn't say anything to them," Gregory said in a small voice. "You can't blame me for it. They overheard us outside." He pointed to Death and Wade.

"I don't know what you're talking about," Mitch said, clasping his hands in front of him on the table. On the outside, he tried to act cool, unaffected. But I could easily see he was peeing himself. He was pale, sweaty, and he kept shifting his gaze to Wade.

"Don't fuckin' bullshit me. You wanna fuck Lucas's life, and I wanna know why. You got a hard-on for Lucas? This a weird way to show you want in his pants."

I screwed up my nose at the mention of Mitch having a hard-on. Thinning my lips, I wanted to know exactly what Wade heard from them outside since he knew Mitch liked to mess with my life.

Mitch scoffed. "Shit no. He's a faggot. I wouldn't touch him, ever."

Oh shit.

Wade grabbed the back of Mitch's head and slammed his face into the table. Mitch screamed and grabbed at his face as blood sprayed from his nose. I caught the librarian coming our way, but Death intercepted her, talking low.

Wade leaned close to Mitch, his voice low and rough, "I like fuckin' guys. You gonna call me a faggot?"

He shook his head and winced. The librarian was buying whatever Death was saying since she wasn't on the phone or looking over here. She was listening to everything Death said and then giggled. Magic again or just Death's charm.

"Then if I ever hear you say that word or any derogatory word like that again, I'll make sure it's not only your nose that's broken. Now fuckin' tell me why you sent fuckface there after Lucas? Why you wanted fuckface to date Lucas?"

"He what?" I breathed.

West tapped my leg. I looked to him, and he shook his head. He wanted me to keep quiet, but heck, I needed answers as well. However, Wade seemed to have it under control, so I sat back and crossed my arms over my chest.

Wade, using his hand on Mitch's neck, shook him a little. "Talk, motherfucker."

Mitch made a noise in the back of his throat. He dropped his hands from his face, exposing the blood dripping out of his nose. "Fine, all right… Lucas has everything I wanted. I was the best at everything until he showed up. Then I was always second best, and it was never enough for my father. 'You should be more like Lucas,' he would say after checking with school about grades and shit to see who was the best." Mitch glared at me. "I wanted one last chance at being better, so I got Gregory to date Lucas, make him fall for him, and then he was supposed to break up with him. Break him. Then I would be on top."

He made me feel sick. I laughed, shaking my head at the fool. "This is why you've been sending death threats to me?"

"What?" Wade snarled.

Mitch glanced from both of us before settling on me. "I didn't send you anything."

I shook my head. "Mitch, I'm not stupid. You know this, and you're the only person who had it out for me, so I know they came from you."

"Why didn't you do anything about them?"

I huffed out a laugh. "They didn't scare me. I knew you wouldn't follow through with them." I left off the "Duh" part. I shook my head again since I couldn't believe what all this was about. I knew, just knew, it would be something silly. "I never got better scores than you on purpose. If you had talked to me, told me what you just said, maybe I would have helped."

Mitch snorted, then cringed. "What? You would have got a lower score?"

I shrugged. "Maybe. But you didn't come to me and tell me what a dick your dad was." Sudden anger had me reaching out and flicking his broken nose. Mitch howled while the others around us chuckled. I would have liked to have done more to him after everything he'd done, but I didn't. Instead, I finished with "If you had been nice, reached out to me, instead of acting as you had, things would have been different. I just hope you learn from all this, and if you still have a problem with me, you need to get over it because I don't want to have to see you again."

West tapped the table. "You mean to tell me jealousy had you be a dick to Lucas for years?" He laughed again. "You're a piece of work." West clapped his hands once. "Wreck, you should beat him up some more. Maybe you'll knock some sense into him."

Wade snorted. "If he's stupid enough to mess with Lucas again, then I will." He leaned closer to Mitch, who flinched. "Are you stupid?"

"No. I won't say or do anything to Lucas again. I promise."

"Smart. Now, whatever you have on Gregory had better disappear or be given back, or that'll piss me off. Do you want to piss me off?"

"No," Mitch said. He opened his mouth and then closed it, then opened it, and asked, "If I pay you, will you kill him?"

We all fell silent.

"What the fuck you askin'?" Wade demanded.

"He… my father," he snarled. "He… lays his hands on my mother and me to… to keep us in line."

My stomach dropped.

It wasn't just about jealousy. He *needed* to be at the top of his classes because he got beat otherwise. My belly twisted in guilt. He was desperate. I could see it in his eyes. Desperate for help.

If I would have known this information, I could have done something—or at least tried to—but Mitch wouldn't have said anything unless he had reached his breaking point. With his words to Wade, they screamed he was finished putting up with what he had and needed to do something, anything.

Wade glanced to Death, who caught his eyes and made his way over after saying something to the librarian. Wade then stood, whispered something to Death and Death nodded.

A moment later, Death looked down at Mitch, grunted at something Wade said, and said to Mitch, "Come out the front. You and I will have a chat."

Mitch got up from his seat and quickly marched from the library, with Death following.

"Thank you," Gregory started. He smiled over at me. "I didn't want to do that, not that I didn't want to ask you out, Lucas, I did, but—"

"I would shut up now," West suggested.

Gregory did as soon as he saw the scowl on Wade's face. His upper lip rose. "I didn't do it for you, and we don't give a fuck what you think. Just stay away from Lucas."

Gregory gulped. "I will." He stood and bowed awkwardly and then grabbed his things and swiftly walked from the room.

Wade sat back down and took one of my hands in both of his. "Don't take that on."

"He's right, Lucas," West put in. "He could have done things differently. He could have gone to the cops. He could have confided in someone, but he didn't."

"I should have—"

Wade tugged on my hand and shook his head. "There's nothin' you could have done. But now we know, we'll do somethin' about it."

My eyes widened. "You will?"

"Even though he's been a motherfucker with you, no one deserves that treatment. Death will take care of it."

Death reappeared. "Yeah, kid, I've got it. Don't you stress."

Dragging in a breath, I nodded. Tension did wash away inside of me because I knew they were right. There was nothing I could have done without the knowledge, but I also knew that they would handle it in the best way they saw fit.

"Okay," I whispered. Wade grinned, happy I trusted they would have things under control.

"Are we going to study still?"

I wasn't really in the mood. I bit my bottom lip and looked down at the books on the table, then up at Wade. What I wanted was to go home with Wade, watch TV, eat, and make out. But I did have a test tomorrow I needed to pass.

"Unfortunately, I still need to get a couple of chapters done."

Wade winked. "Death and I will head to the burger joint, hang out for a few hours, and then I'll bring you something back."

Never had I expected Wade could be like this. To me, that was the sweetest thing he could have done.

"Okay," I said softly.

"Fuck," he clipped. He glanced at West. "Make sure you're with him all the damn time. I'm sure you know by now he goes into a bubble where nothin' but what's in front of him can penetrate."

He said penetrate. With my mood somewhat lifted, I wanted to laugh like a little twelve-year-old.

West did it for me and muttered, "He said penetrate."

Wade made a noise in the back of his throat while Death chuckled.

West sobered. "Got it, big guy. I'm on Lucas watch, and I won't let you down."

"You know I am here and can take care of myself, right?" I asked. They all looked at me and smiled. I rolled my eyes and threw my hands up, grumbling, "Whatever."

"Can you bring something back for me?" West asked.

"No," Wade replied sharply.

"Wade," I said.

Death laughed. "Don't worry, kid, I'll bring your friend back some food."

"Thank you, Death," I told him.

"Lucas, see me out," Wade ordered. When I didn't move, his gaze narrowed. "Please."

"Hooey, look at that, men. Wreck said please. Kid, you must be amazin' in bed to tame the grump," Death teased, and earned a scowl from Wreck where I just went bright red.

"Do not say that shit, brother," Wade warned.

Death grinned like it didn't sound like Wade was ready to rip him a new asshole.

West leaned into me and whispered, "Are you sure with him?"

Wade's hard gaze shot to him, then to me. I smiled and said, "Yes." It was then Wade smiled back at me.

I took Lucas's hand as we walked out of the library. "I'll be back by ten, that all right?" I asked. I turned into him, resting my hands on his waist, and he dropped his to my upper arms.

"Sounds good, but you know you don't have to come back, right?"

I glared down at him. "Do you not want me to?"

"No, I—"

"Did that shit scare you? What I did? I didn't know his father did shit to him, or I wouldn't have put my fuckin' hands on him. But I had to make sure he understood you were off-limits."

"I know, it's not—"

I dropped my hands, second-guessing myself and finding that I'd never done that with anyone in the past, but I didn't want Lucas to be pissed at me for anything, or disgusted. Shit, I was a goner for this guy. I didn't realize how much.

"I can try to change—"

His hand slapped over my mouth. "Holy heck, Wade. Let me talk." He smiled. That was a good sign. My body relaxed a little. "I don't want you to change. I like you as you are. You're protective, I understand that. It can be scary to see you in your… ah, Avenger mode, but it's also…." He trailed off, and with the streetlights showing and the ones shining through the library window, I could see him blushing.

"Also what?" I asked after removing his hand and holding it in mine to keep in one place since he looked ready to bolt with how many times he kept glancing back to the library doors.

He rolled his eyes. "You know."

"Don't have a clue." I did, and I suspected he knew I knew, but I also wanted him to say it.

He sighed. "A turn-on," he blurted quickly and went to turn to run off.

Laughing, I grabbed him around the waist and spun him back into me. "You're too fuckin' cute. I'm messin' with you, but I'm glad you think it's a turn-on. Everythin' you do seems to get me hard."

"Oh" was all he said. Yet, I felt how he stilled, saw his eyes widen, and watched as his blush deepened.

"And what the fuck is Avenger's mode?"

His brows shot up. "You don't know Avengers? The movies? Or even Captain America?" I shook my head. "Thor?"

"Haven't a damn clue."

"Wade, we're going to have to watch them together."

Shit, I'd sit through any movie with Lucas at my side. "Sounds like a date."

He bit his bottom lip, but I caught his smile. "I'd like that."

"Then it's done." I tugged at the neck of his turtleneck, and he was quick to glare up at me.

"Yes, let's talk about that. I had to hide a hickey, Wade. If my brother saw that, then he would ask questions, and I'm not really good at lying. If you're going to leave something behind, can you make it on other parts of my body?" he flushed, no doubt realizing what he'd just asked for.

Grinning, I told him, "I can do that."

"Um… well, then… okay."

I didn't want to go, but the quicker he studied, the quicker I could come back for him. Why did two hours seem like a fucking long time all of a sudden? "Gotta get there to get back and feed you. Now kiss me, Lucas."

"Okay," he whispered. He reached up, curled his arms around my neck, and I dipped enough to have his mouth in a hard, deep kiss.

"You know you guys can make out later, right? I'm starvin'," Death called.

I cursed under my breath as I tucked Lucas's hair behind his ear. "Stay in there until I come back. And trust me when I say we'll deal with fuckhead's father."

His smile was soft, his eyes warm, and fuck me did I want to see what he looked like after I fucked him. He nodded. "I will and I do trust you."

My chest swelled. Christ, he made me happy. "Good." I gave him a quick peck and walked off to my bike, where a grinning-like-a-fucking-idiot Death stood leaning against his. I glanced back to make sure Lucas had gone in, but he was still standing there. I shot him a chin lift. He gave me a wave, then turned around and disappeared through the doors.

"Holy fuck, you two are lost in each other. I don't know if I should kill you to take your place or throw the fuck up because it's so adorable."

"Shut the fuck up," I clipped, without any real bite. I hadn't felt this damn good in a long time.

Lucas did that to me.

Yeah, there was no way in fuck I was giving that up.

"We gettin' food, or you wanna stalk him from out here?"

"Food," I stated but glanced back again.

Death laughed. "Are you sure?"

"Get the hell on your ride, brother."

LUCAS

As soon as I was inside, I knew I would get the fifth degree from West. At least I had the glow of kissing Wade outside to get me through it. Well, I hoped.

What added to the glow was how he'd been worried what I thought of him with how he dealt with Mitch. It was sweet he'd been concerned. It showed me he cared.

It was only the second day for us. It was new and exciting learning about one another. But it also felt comfortable…. Mostly when I wasn't getting embarrassed by something I'd done or things he said. Like how I gave him a hard-on all the time. Heck, I wanted to fan myself over that line.

I managed to make it to the table and sit before West demanded, "Everything."

Shrugging, I pulled my books over to me and said, "There's not much to say— Ow, dang it. That hurt," I told him, rubbing my shin.

"Well, don't leave me hanging. Lucas, he's one large, scary mofo, and cranky seems to be his middle name. Did you see the way he just banged assface's head into the table without a thought? I mean, yes, it's bad what he has to deal with, with his dad, but he shouldn't have messed with you. At least we know they'll handle it and get Mitch out of shit." He took a breath and went on. "Then, when Wreck looks at you, it's like everything slows down, and all his attention goes on to you. It's amazing, and I'm totally jealous."

My heart raced in my chest from West's intake of Wade and me. I hadn't noticed, yet now he'd painted the picture, I could see it clearly. My emotions latched on, telling me I liked him so much more than the first day.

West chuckled. "You hadn't seen it?"

"No," I admitted. "I keep worrying this will all just be a phase for him, but then he says or does something to make me forget that worry and I want to believe. I really want to believe."

He tapped his foot against mine. I looked up at him to find him smiling. "I think you can continue to believe because from what I've seen, and it's only been a short time, is that he's completely taken with you. How did you get so lucky?"

I rolled my eyes, but I couldn't wipe the grin from my face because I did feel lucky. "Come on, you have something good going on with—"

"We broke up," he announced.

"Wait, what?"

"Shush," the librarian called out.

"When, how, why?"

When his lips thinned, but I caught the tremble beforehand, I knew it was bad. He glanced away and then back again with watery eyes.

"West," I uttered. "What happened?"

He shook his head and sniffed. "Nothing. I don't want to talk about it." He laughed. "I was going to cancel coming tonight, but I'm glad I didn't, or I would have missed out on all this excitement."

"West," I tried again.

"It helped keep my mind off things."

What had the… the bastard done to my best friend?

"Do I need Wade to beat Sam up? I'll ask, just for you, if it'll make you feel better."

West laughed. "No. Well… maybe, I'll keep the offer in mind."

"You know I'm here for you?"

West nodded. "I know."

"Did he hurt you?"

He sniffed again and looked down at the table. "Only emotionally." He took a deep breath. "I caught him sleeping with someone else."

Anger burned inside me. From the couple of times I'd met Sam, I'd thought he was a good one. West had been so taken with him. My heart ached for my friend.

"Do you know what this calls for?" I asked.

He rubbed at his eyes. "What?"

"Swear words." I sucked in a breath. "That motherfucking butt-hole, prick, donkey-nose bastard deserves his dick to rot and fall off."

West's eyes widened, and then he laughed. "Jesus, no wonder you don't swear. Donkey-nose bastard." He smiled. "Thank you, Lucas. You're a good friend."

I shrugged.

"Now, do you know what would distract me even more?"

"What?" Although, I had a feeling it was something to do with Wade and me.

"Telling me about kissing that fine man of yours."

Called it.

In the end, I only gave West a few details. I wanted to make him feel better, after all. But I kept the main parts to myself. I was greedy and didn't want to share what had happened between us. Even when it had been only once.

Eventually, he realized I would keep being evasive on the more important details, so we got our heads stuck into studying. It wasn't until a hand slapped to the table right next to me that I woke from my zone.

"What?" I asked, blinking up and around me.

West stood beside me, Wade on the other side.

"It's a sickness," West said with a shake of his head and a laugh. "But that's how I've learned to get his attention," West explained to Wade.

"To scare him."

"Yep, unless he comes out of it on his own, but he won't do that until he's finished."

"It's a worry," Wade commented.

"Don't stress. Usually when he's out studying, someone's with him." His hands shot up. "I'm not talking about on a date or a guy who wants to bone him. Though there are a few."

"Give me their fuckin' names," Wade clipped.

I quickly stood and grabbed his arm. "He's only teasing. There aren't any." I glared over my shoulder at a smirking West. Glancing back to Wade, I boldly rested my hand against his neck. His eyes dropped to me. "Did you bring food?"

He picked up his hand and rattled the paper bag. "Got it here."

"Great, should I eat here or home?"

He smiled. "Up to you."

"Did West get any?"

"Got my bag here, and I'm going to head home to eat it."

Facing him, I asked, "Do you want to come to my place? We can… have a drink or something?"

He smiled. "Sweet of you to ask, but I'll be fine. Go and have fun with your guy while your brother's out working."

Of course, heat hit my cheeks. I'd told him about us not saying anything to Zion until we were steady in the relationship. I'd forgotten for a moment Zion wasn't going to be home so the thought of going there with Wade alone had my lower stomach tingling.

"West, I'd like you to come," I tried again, worried about him going to his apartment alone. I quickly placed my books in my backpack before looking to West again.

"Stop, I'm not going to go home and cry into my Wheaties. I'll be fine. Now, I'm heading off. Thanks for the entertainment and have a good night." He made his way to the door and headed out.

I kind of felt guilty because I didn't press more.

"What happened?"

Sighing, I turned back to Wade. "He caught his boyfriend cheating. He really cared for him, so it's a terrible situation he's in."

"Shit."

"Yeah. I don't know what this will do to him."

"All you can do is be there for him," Wade said as he took my hand, and I grabbed my bag off the table. "But if you want, we can go to his place and check on him."

That was so darn sweet.

Smiling up at him, I shook my head. "He's just left and said he didn't need company. I'll leave it for tonight but then call him tomorrow." We walked outside hand in hand, and I couldn't help but stare down at his palm in mine.

He was holding my hand in public.

Like we'd been doing it forever.

"How are you so comfortable to hold my hand?"

When we stopped at a car, he pressed my back into it and loomed over me. "Because it's you. I'm findin' I don't give a fuck what people think when it comes to this because it feels natural. I still wanna keep things between us for a while. Is that cool?"

"Yeah, it is." Anything he said right then I would be cool with it. Having Wade "Wreck" Williams stare down at me like I was the only thing in his world was everything I could have wished for.

Never had I thought my lust-filled fantasy would come true. This straight man was telling me he wanted me. Was barricading me in his arms as I leaned against the car and grinned like a maniac up at him.

Maybe I would buy a lotto ticket because it seemed my luck was changing.

"What are you thinkin'?" he asked, his voice low and rough.

"How lucky I am," I blurted without thinking and then thought I sounded like such a fool.

He smiled but shook his head. "I'm the lucky one."

My phone vibrated in my pocket. Wade pulled back and said, "Check it. Could be Saint sayin' he's not workin' but comin' home."

True, but I hoped it wasn't. Wade pulled keys out, and the car behind me unlocked. I turned, looking at it. "I thought you had your bike."

He opened the door for me. "Know you're not a fan yet. Thought you'd prefer a lift home in this instead of you walking and me following you on the bike."

My heart melted into a gooey pile inside me.

"That's, um, very nice," I said softly as I slid into my seat.

He leaned in and kissed me quickly before straightening and

walking around the car to the driver side. Of course, I watched the show in front of me, until my phone sounded again, notifying me I had an unread message.

Mom: Hello, my sweeties, just to let you know your aunt's procedure is getting delayed a month. Looks like we won't be back this weekend (crying emoji). I'm blaming your father. He did this somehow. I miss both of my boys so much.

When Wade was seated and had started the car, I told him, "It's Mom. They were supposed to come home this weekend for a while to help an aunt out, but it's been delayed," I explained, then snorted at Zion's comment in the group chat, which I told Wade as well.

Zion: But you miss me more than Lucas, right?

Mom: I don't have favorites. Well, except if our little Muffy was still alive, then she would be my favorite.

Zion: Seriously, Mom, you would pick a mutt called Muffy over your own sons?

Mom: Yes (smiley winky face)

Zion: Do you know what muff stands for, Mom?

Dad: She found out when I said I wanted to eat hers (laughing emoji). She got scared I meant the dog.

Me: DAD TMI!!!!

Zion: Dad, no, just no.

Mom: Gerry, you're sleeping on the couch tonight!

Dad: Come on, Lucy, it's not like they haven't done it.... Well, except maybe Lucas. Son, have you ever been with a woman?

I gasped. "Holy heck."

"What?" Wade asked. Thankfully I'd stopped reading the comments after Mom's one about the dog. This was just embarrassing.

Me: OMG I am NOT talking about this or anything sexual related to either of my parents. Anyway, I've got studying to do, miss you, talk soon, but never about this again.

Mom: See, Gerry you've scared him off now.

I closed the group message down and groaned. Sometimes my

parents just went too far. It was lucky I loved them, because I knew they meant well in the end.

"Lucas, you're bright red. What's going on?" he asked, trying not to smile.

Sighing, I placed a hand over my eyes and told him what Dad asked. I didn't have to wait. As soon as I spoke, Wade chuckled. It was when he quickly sobered, I removed my hand to see his tight grip on the wheel.

"What?" I asked.

"Nothin," he replied, his voice a little tight.

"Wade, tell me."

He glanced at me then back at the road just before he slowed and pulled up out the front of Zion's house. "I just don't like the thought of you being with anyone."

Oh, wow. He was jealous.

I wasn't sure if I could do it, but I sucked up my nerves and reached out with a shaky hand to place it on his thigh. "I've had one experience, and it wasn't the best." He went to open his mouth, but I got there first with "You're older. I know you've been with many women, and numbers don't matter to me because I know you're here with me, and that's all that matters."

His jaw clenched as he flung his door open and got out.

Had I said something wrong?

CHAPTER SIXTEEN
WRECK

uck me. *Fuck me.* My chest felt thick, like my heart had swelled so damn big. I took a gulp of cool night air and rubbed a hand over my face.

I know you're here with me, and that's all that matters.

His words were the most perfect thing I'd ever heard. It meant he didn't give a shit about my past and the number of women I'd fucked. He wasn't scared I was playing him, and those words proved it. He knew I was where I wanted to be.

Walking around the car, I opened his door, leaned in, and undid his seat belt.

"Did I say something wrong?" he asked quietly.

"No," I clipped. I shifted back, and Lucas got out of the car. When he was out of the way, I slammed the door closed and locked it. I grabbed the keys and his bag out of Lucas's hand and then stalked up to the front door. I knew I was being weird, cold even, but I just needed to get him inside with the door closed and locked behind us.

Unlocking the front door, I pushed it wide, stepped in, dumped his backpack on the ground and waited for Lucas to step through. He did with a frown and drawn brows. He was worried. I didn't like

I'd made him worry, but he would soon know why I was being a dickhead.

Closing the door, I locked it, and faced him. Only he had his back to me and seemed to be looking around the living room while wringing his hands.

Shit, I'd gone and fucked this up. I stepped up to his side, grabbed his wrist gently, and led him down the hall to his bedroom. He followed, and I was surprised, yet grateful, he did. Inside the room, I turned him, cupped his cheeks, and kissed him.

Seconds.

That was all it took for Lucas to melt into me and accept my kiss, give it back, and turn it into more when his mouth opened against mine. I gripped his turtleneck and tugged it up. We broke apart enough for me to pull it from his body, then we were back to kissing. Lucas fumbled with my vest, and then it slid down my arms. The frantic kissing stopped. I took the vest and placed it on the office chair in his room. Turning back to him, I gripped my long-sleeved top and dragged it off my body, throwing it to the floor.

I then took in Lucas. His chest rose and fell rapidly. His pale skin outshone the backdrop of his bedroom, and I wanted to taste every inch. He wasn't bulky like I was. He was slim but firm. Shit, the six-pack surprised me.

His cheeks heated under my gaze, and I watched as his eyes darted over my upper body. He went to cross his arms over his chest, and I wondered if he felt inadequate next to my larger, broader frame. I didn't want him to because, to me, he was fuckin' perfect.

"Don't," I ordered. "Don't hide. Ever. I've never got hard for a guy, never thought about a guy, and look at me here in your room, wanting you. You're fuckin' stunnin', Lucas."

He rolled his eyes.

"Do I need to prove how stunnin' I think you are?" I stepped closer, my cock throbbing under my jeans. Shit, every time I thought of this guy, I was sporting a semi or instantly hard.

He shrugged.

Good, I'd show him by my actions.

I'd never thought about doing this before to anyone, but I couldn't wait to taste Lucas. Stopping in front of him, he smiled shyly. Only when I dropped to my knees, his mouth popped open in shock, and his eyes widened.

"What are you doing?" he asked, his voice high from shock. He tried to pull me back up, but I wouldn't move.

"Provin' to you how much I like your body."

"Oh my God, you… ah, you don't have to do that." He fought me as I undid his jeans button and lowered his zipper.

"Know I don't have to, Lucas, but want to."

His hands landed over mine at his waist just as I hooked two fingers in to tug them down. "Stop, I… you're, um, new to this… ah, it, you might not like it, and then you'll leave."

That was what he was worried about? Shit, he didn't need to concern himself.

A chuckle dropped from my lips, and I shook my head. He seriously had no idea how much I craved his body.

"Lucas."

"Y-Yes?"

"Remove your hands."

"But—"

"Lucas, now," I clipped.

He swallowed thickly and removed his hands from over mine, resting them down at his sides. I liked seeing his erratic breathing as I slowly glided his pants down his legs and helped him kick them off. His already hard dick sprang free and bounced in front of me, as if begging me to taste it.

I couldn't wait.

I placed my hands at the back of Lucas's thighs and rubbed them up over his ass cheeks. He shivered and panted, looking down at me with desire in his eyes.

I kissed his hip, then the other. "You're fuckin' sexy, Lucas." I licked the tip of his leaking cock, and he moaned my name. Christ, I liked hearing it. "You want my mouth?"

"Yes," he whispered.

"You got it," I told him, and sucked the first cock I'd ever had into my mouth. His smooth skin tasted salty, but it was a good kind. I licked, sucked, and slid my mouth, tongue, and lips up and down his shaft.

"Wade," he cried. "So close."

I tightened my grip on his ass cheeks and pushed his hips forward, making his cock push into my mouth. I glanced up to see the wonderment in his eyes. He slowly shifted his hips back and then forced his dick in. His eyes darkened, his mouth opened, and then he dropped his head back and groaned.

He looked back down at me, then out into the room. "Oh God," he cried just as he pushed all the way in and came down my throat. He covered his face with his hands and mumbled something.

Grinning, I stood and removed his hands, but then he buried his face into my chest. "What did you say?"

He shook his head.

"Lucas" was all I said.

"That was the hottest thing I've ever seen," he blurted. "But I came in like two seconds."

My chest shook with my laugh. "It's good to see I can make you crazy like you do me," I told him. He let out a squeal as I picked him up. He locked his legs around my waist, and I carried him to his bed. I sat, his legs untangling around me, so I lay back and kicked my feet up, rearranging him over my body.

Picking up the cover, I flicked it over his bare back. He got to his hands over me and stared down. "What's this?"

"Sleep time."

"You…." He shook his head. "No."

"No?" I smiled. "Why?"

He ground his ass into my still hard cock. "Because of that."

"It'll go away. I wanted you to know what your words meant to me and how much I fuckin' love your body. Now it's time to rest."

His eyes warmed. "Was that all the macho actions outside? I thought I'd said something wrong."

"You didn't. You couldn't. I find you too fuckin' adorable."

He glared down at me, and I wanted to laugh. Fuck, he was cute. Reaching up, I tucked his hair behind an ear.

"I'm not adorable. Cute is okay, but not adorable," he stated.

Smirking, I said, "Sure."

He rolled his eyes, and I couldn't stop looking at him. Fuck, he made me feel so much.

He rocked against me again, and I gripped his hips to stop while I ground my teeth together. Christ, I wanted to slide my cock right into what I knew would be a tight hole, but I didn't want to rush this.

Hell, that was a first. Usually I'd have a woman under me in a second, but I didn't want that with Lucas.

Motherfucking hell, he was making me mushy.

"Let's get some sleep."

When he pouted, I grabbed the back of his head and dragged him down so I could kiss that pout right off his lips. Only he thought I was giving him the go-ahead, so he rubbed his body up and down over me.

"Stop," I ordered.

"Wade," he said, kissing my neck.

"Yeah?"

"Can I ask a favor?"

"Uh-huh."

"I want to suck your cock," he whispered into my ear.

My hands tightened, one in his hair, the other at his waist. "You undo me, Lucas Storey."

I felt his smile against my cheek before his kiss. He shifted back and said, "Please?"

"Never beg for anythin' from me, Lucas. You can have anythin' you want."

He pulled back, and I got to see his smile; it was damn beautiful. He kissed my chest, licked, and then sucked on my nipple. I hissed out a breath and cupped the back of his head.

Lucas paused and grinned. "Hands behind your head. No touching. Just see and feel."

Christ, it was going to be a challenge since I fucking loved touching him, but I'd give it a go. I placed my hands behind my head and let Lucas have his fun. He kissed me quickly and went back to taking his time on both nipples.

It was so damn hard not to reach out for him. Just watching and feeling was different. No woman had asked that of me. They'd been greedy in wanting everything, but then there was Lucas. Wanting to give and shit, maybe it was because I'd already drunk his cum down…. Ah, fuck, who cared what it was. I was close to forgetting my own name when Lucas dipped lower and kissed me just above my jeans.

"Lucas," I warned, close to jizzing in my pants before he even got there. Fuck, it had never been this intense before.

Grinning, he met my eyes and undid the button, then slowly unzipped me. He dipped again and kissed my dick over my boxers. He grabbed my jeans, and I lifted my ass so he could pull them down. He shifted out of the way so he could take them all the way off, along with my boxers and socks, before he moved back between my legs.

"I like this view," he said softly, his cheeks heating again. Goddamn, he was innocent and sweet.

"Glad you like it, Lucas. I like mine as well."

And I did. Seeing him naked between my legs, his wild hair everywhere, his plump lips redder than usual, and knowing I got him off, was a shot right to the cock.

Smiling shyly, he lay on his belly, but up on his elbows, and brought my dick to his mouth to press a kiss to the tip. I clenched my jaw when he licked around the mushroom head and then sucked on it.

"Lucas, you gotta give it to me before I lose control and roll you over so *I* can fuck your mouth."

My dick slid from his mouth, and his lips were still parted in an O shape.

Fuck me, he wanted that. There went another shot to my cock.

Growling in the back of my throat, I sat up quickly, grabbed Lucas under the arms, picked him up, and flung him back on the bed. In the next second, I was up and hovering over him with my dick dangling right near his mouth.

"Open for me, Lucas," I ordered roughly, gliding the tip of my dick over his lips.

He moaned and opened his mouth while he used one hand to grab the back of my thigh and the other to glide up and down my chest, as if encouraging me to fuck his face.

"Jesus," I hissed and pushed my dick into his warm, wet heat. His lips clamped down around me, eager to suck. As I pulled out slowly, I used one hand to cup the back of his head and adjust it for the right angle. I pistoned in and out, testing and feeling how fucking amazing it was. His mouth was to die for.

When I glanced down, I near blacked out from the pleasure coursing through me. Not only was Lucas taking my thrusting, opening his throat to me without gagging, but he loved it. He had his hand on his own cock, knees bent as he ran his palm up and down in a fast rhythm.

"Fucking hell." I ground my teeth together so I wouldn't lose my load. But then Lucas slid his hand from my thigh to cup my balls, and right away, they drew up into my body as if he'd commanded them. "Fuck," I bit out. "Your mouth feels damn good."

I lifted his head a little and fucked his mouth over and over. My body tingled for God's sake. I knew I was going to lose my load and do it hard.

When Lucas hummed around me and then moaned, I glanced back down to see his cum shoot out and land over his pale skin.

"Christ, I'm gonna come. Want me to move?" His answer was to grip me tighter with his hands at the back of my thighs again. He didn't want me to go anywhere.

I stared down at him as I let out a deep groan when the first squirt of cum shot into his mouth. He took it and drank it down, then again when more came from my body.

Breathing hard, I withdrew my dick slowly, and Lucas licked it all the way around. Then before I sat back, he grabbed my cock, drawing the last drop out of the tip onto his tongue before swallowing it.

"Fucking hell," I muttered. "That was damn hot." Of course, he blushed. But a man loved when it felt like their person couldn't get enough of their partner's load and wanted more. I dropped to the bed, reached to the bedside table and grabbed a wad of tissues which I used to clean Lucas up with, then threw them to the floor.

"Come here," I ordered with my arm outstretched.

He moved around and curled into my side with his head on my shoulder and arm over my waist.

"You like being controlled in bed, Lucas?" From what I could see, he did, but he also liked soft and sweet.

"Sometimes," he mumbled.

"Good."

"Um, can you tell me something about yourself? Unless you want to sleep. I mean, I know we rushed into that, but I didn't expect the reaction you had from what I'd said, and it went kind of crazy from there—not that I'm complaining because I'm not. I liked it, ah, a lot. So, um, if you're tired, we can talk another time."

Chuckling, I gave him a squeeze and said, "I'll talk, but I want you to eat while I do. Shit, we didn't even bring in the food from the car." I shifted him over and sat up. Reaching for my jeans, I pulled them on. "I'll go get it. Don't fuckin' move, and then we'll talk."

"Okay," he whispered, and I knew when he whispered like that, he was feeling whatever I'd said or was going to do deeply.

I liked that.

CHAPTER SEVENTEEN
LUCAS

The next morning, I was in the kitchen cooking bacon and eggs and thinking about the night before. We'd stayed up late getting to know one another. We didn't have many things in common, but we still fit. He liked outdoor things, where I would prefer anything inside. However, relationships were about compromise. When I told him that, while looking like a fire engine with how red I was, I said I would be willing to try things he enjoyed. He took my mouth like he needed it to breathe.

What I enjoyed was there was no pressure of when we'd sleep together. I didn't mean in the same bed. We'd done that last night, and I enjoyed it 100 percent, but I thought Wade would have wanted to progress quickly. He didn't; he was happy to get to know one another and fool around before we moved on.

Honestly, I couldn't deny my emotions. My heart was already committed to Wade Williams.

It was scary.

I could get hurt.

But I wanted to take the chance for him. Even if I tried, I couldn't back away from him now. Not when he'd shown me how sweet he could be with me.

Hands settled on my waist. I dropped the tongs and turned to wrap my arms around his neck.

"Morning," I muttered, noticing he was fully dressed.

He grunted while gifting me with warm, tired eyes and a small smile. Apparently, he wasn't a morning person. The knowledge made my smile grow.

Lifting to my toes, I pressed my mouth against his. "I'll get you a coffee."

He grunted again and kissed my neck, where he'd marked me, before moving to rest his jean-clad ass against the counter.

"Breakfast is nearly done. We should have it all away and us showered by the time Zion gets home from work," I told him as I puttered around. "Are you sure you want to watch *Avengers* here with Zion in his room sleeping?" Wade had said the previous night, when I went on and on about how good *Avengers* was, that he wanted to see it today.

"Yeah, Lucas. You tell me when he crashes, and I'll come back."

"Sounds like a plan," I said, handing him his coffee. He dipped down again for a quick kiss, and then I moved back to the pan.

"Need a hand?" he asked.

"I've got it," I answered and dished up the meals. We sat at the table, and I couldn't stop looking at him enjoying the meal I made. This was what made it all seem real. Wade was in the house after staying the night, and we were doing what boyfriends did with each other.

"What are you thinkin'?" he asked, his brow quirked.

I finished what I was chewing and shrugged. "Um, just that, ah, this, what we're doing, it feels real."

He cocked his head to the side. "Real?"

I shook my head. "I mean, I know it's real, you and me, but this sitting here with you after you sleeping over has me believing we're actually in a relationship—that is if you, I… ah, as long as you think we are, then I'm, um, cool with it. If you don't, then, ah, I'm okay with that also." He stared at me. I sighed. "To be honest, I won't be okay with it. I would like to name it and say we *are* in a relationship… if that's okay with you?"

He grinned, and my chest stopped with its compression. "It's what I want, so yeah, Lucas, we're in a relationship."

"Well, okay," I said quietly because my body was refilling with all its gooey, mushy feelings.

A phone chimed. Wade pulled it out of his back pocket. "Fuck," he clipped and then looked up at me. "Saint's on his way back now. Death just told me."

"Crap!" I cried and quickly grabbed up our plates and took them to the kitchen. I rushed around like a mad man and got things cleaned. I'd even taken Wade's coffee from him and dumped the rest down the drain to put the mug in the dishwasher along with the other items.

"I hate this," Wade said from behind me, causing me to jump.

With a hand to my heart, I spun around. "You scared me, and what do you hate?"

He was already fully dressed. "Sneakin'. I'd like to stay."

"We'll get there."

"I know. Now kiss me and then text me when he's gone to sleep." He stepped close, only to pause and angle his head toward the front of the house. "Fuck, he's here already."

My eyes widened, and my heart gave off a nervous flutter. "What will we do? Your car's in the driveway."

"Shit. All right, relax. Just relax." He rubbed my arms up and down. "Let me handle it."

"Okay, yep, good, I'm terrible at acting."

The front door unlocked. Wade leaned in, kissed me quickly, and said, "Since I don't have a coffee now, pretend you're gettin' me one."

I practically ran to the coffee pot and pressed it on just as the door opened, and Zion called, "Yo, what are you doin' here, brother?" He dumped his things on the table by the door and moved our way.

Before Wade had the chance to answer, I opened my mouth with "Good morning to you, Zion. I had a great night, how about yourself?" I lowered my voice and pretended to be Zion, "Well, Lucas, my night wasn't too bad, thanks for asking." I heard Wade mutter something, and I quickly shut my mouth, only to open it and ask, "I'm just making a coffee. Do you want one?" I glanced back to see Zion had stopped and was looking at me like I'd grown another head overnight. "What?"

"You a bit buzzed there, bro? Maybe you don't need any more coffee. How about I get it?"

"No, I've got it. Are you going to bed?" I blurted, and mentally cursed myself because it sounded like I was eager to get rid of him.

Zion's brows dipped. "What happened to you? Wait… holy fuck." He stomped forward, grabbed my chin, and turned my head. "Who in the hell gave you a hickey? Is that why you're actin' weird? Is that Gregory guy still here?"

Wade made a noise in the back of his throat, and Zion went to look at him, but I yelled, "What? Ha, yeah, no, I mean, I got the hickey, but he's gone. Long gone."

Zion's eyes narrowed. "Did that fucker hurt you? Did he tag, bag, and run? I'll kill him if he hurt your feelin's."

I laughed, only it was forced. "No feelings were hurt. It, ah, just didn't work out for us."

"Really?" he asked.

"Yes. Now you don't need to hunt him down."

Zion turned to Wade. "Did you see the guy leave?"

"No," he bit out.

"What are you doin' here?" Zion questioned, crossing his arms over his chest.

"Food," I yelled. They both looked at me. "Anyone hungry? I can make some, um, stuff."

"I ate on the way home," Zion said.

"I'm good," Wade answered, his voice lighter, probably from

being amused by me. I'd told him I was terrible at acting. I was so going to get us caught out.

"I stopped in to try and catch you before you crashed," Wade told him. "Wanted to see how the night went."

"All right," Zion drew out. I could tell from his tone he was suspicious.

"Was gonna make an ad for the position you were talkin' about. Wanted to run it by you," Wade added, cottoning on to Zion's suspicion.

"Right, yeah, an ad would be good. I tried to come up with one but wasn't sure statin' we're lookin' for guys to do guys and gals was good."

Wade chuckled. "Doubt it."

"So, you're going to add men to the Polished Pussy?"

"Shit, now you said that, what about the name? We'll need to add somethin' to it, so people know men are available as well."

"Polished Pussies and Penises," I said, more to myself than the other two.

Zion clapped, I jumped, and my brother grinned. "That's it. All we need to add is 'and penises.' It'll be simple. There's room on the buildin'." He punched me in the arm. "Good thinkin', bro."

"Well, I'll get out of here and get an ad started. I'll also contact a signwriter to change the name."

"Sounds good." Zion nodded.

"Coffee," I announced, blushing when they both looked at me. "Um, no one has had any."

Zion shook his head. "I'm good. It'll keep me up if I have one now."

"Another time," Wade said with a small smile.

I didn't want him to go, but I knew he had to or else it would look suss he stayed while his friend went to bed, leaving him alone with me, someone he supposedly didn't know much about.

"Right, okay." I nodded. "I'm going for a shower then." Wade's jaw clenched. Was he thinking about me naked in the shower? "Um, bye." I waved to Wade.

"Later," he called.

"Hey, bro, wake me about five, yeah?"

"Yep, got it, five." *Now hurry up and get to bed so Wade can come back.*

When I heard the front door being unlocked, my stomach swirled in excitement. Wade was back. I jumped up from the couch where I'd been studying and quickly raced over. Only when the door opened, my grin faded when I saw not only Wade but Death and Kylo as well.

"Hey, kid," Death said, stepping into the house.

"Um… hi to all of you."

"Kylo overheard me and Wreck talkin' about watchin' those movies you were goin' on about and wanted to join."

Kylo laughed. "Still can't believe they haven't seen *Avengers*. Crazy, right?" He walked by me with his arms full of pizza.

Death moved closer. "Go and calm your man down before he rips Kylo a new asshole."

I could see the scowl on Wade's face, which was directed to Kylo. Before blood was spilled, I said, "Um, Wreck, I need to show you that app on my phone I was telling you about." I gestured toward my room. "It'll only take a moment, but my phone's in my room."

"What app?" Kylo asked. He dumped the pizzas on the coffee table and went to move over near us again.

Death stepped in his path. "You and me, we gotta talk."

Kylo glanced at Death, then me, then Wade, and finally back to Death. I knew he hadn't worked anything out because he still looked confused with his brows drawn.

"Sure," Kylo said, sounding very unsure.

Wade stepped in, closed the door, and with his hand on my

lower back, he moved us down the hall and into my room. There he closed the door before turning to me.

"Fuckin' prospect," he complained as he pulled me into his arms. He dipped his head to bury his nose into my neck, where he drew in a large breath. "Crazy how a person can miss someone even after a few hours."

I wrapped my arms around his waist. "I know what you mean."

Groaning, he lifted his head and pressed a kiss to my temple. "We're goin' to have to watch these movies with Death and the prospect."

"I know. But are you okay doing it without killing Kylo?"

His jaw clenched. "As long as you're sittin' next to me, I might be able to manage to stop spillin' blood."

Chuckling, I said, "I better make sure I'm next to you then."

"It would be wise."

"Okay," I whispered.

He groaned. "Don't say okay like that because every time you do, I want to kiss you."

"Then kiss me," I told him on a whisper, and he did. I gripped him tighter to me as his hand threaded through my hair he loved so much, and we deepened the kiss, leaving us both panting at the end.

"Fuck," he uttered, resting his forehead against mine. "Come on, we'd better get out there."

"Boo." I smiled.

I was glad to have made him laugh before we left the room. With the kiss and the laugh, he looked less like he was willing to murder someone.

Wade dropped my hand at the end of the hall, and we entered the living room. Only I stopped as soon as I saw Kylo. His eyes were wide, and he sat on the chair stiffly.

I glanced at Death. He was sitting in the other chair, leaving the couch for me and Wade. As I moved over to sit by Wade, I watched Kylo's gaze shift from me to Wade and back again many times.

Sighing, I sat down, making sure to leave enough room between Wade and me, then looked at Kylo. "Death told you?"

Death gasped. "What? I would never."

"Fuckin' hell," Wade clipped.

"How... when... how?" Kylo muttered. He rubbed at his eyes. "Was he serious?" he asked, pointing at Death.

"What did he say?" I asked. For once, I wasn't nervous about the outcome. I didn't really want to hide things from Kylo because he was a friend. The only one who couldn't know, who could cause problems for Wade and me was Zion. That was if he didn't like Wade for me.

"That you two are... together?"

I didn't get to reply because in the next moment, I had an arm around my waist, and I was being pulled sideways into a large body. "Yes," Wade said roughly. "And if Saint finds out because of you, I'll fuckin' make sure you regret it."

Grinning up at Wade, I patted his thigh. "Kylo won't say anything."

Wade glanced down at me, his eyes softened, and he tipped his head down to give me a quick kiss. I curled into Wade more and brought my feet up onto the couch while his arm wound around my shoulders.

Kylo was still staring at us, his mouth open in shock.

"I... never... when?" he got out.

"After the party at the compound," I told him.

He jerked his head back. "When I told you there wouldn't be a chance?" Wade growled under his breath. Kylo's hand shot up. "Wait... was he the guy West said to forget about when you went on that date with Gregory?"

Holy God, he was just trying to get himself killed.

Wade had tensed beside me. I pressed into him more in case he thought to jump the coffee table to kick Kylo's butt. Rubbing up and down Wade's thigh, I said, "Yes, but that... look, um, let's not talk about that. Just know we're, ah, seeing each other and that my brother can't know just yet because all this is new, and I don't want anything to come between us." I smiled. "Can you do that? Keep it from Zion?"

Kylo glanced between us, and then finally nodded. "But…" He ground his teeth together. "Even if this gets me beat up." He looked to Wade. "If you hurt him, I'll find a way to make you pay."

It was a tense moment for a while as Wade just sat there glaring at Kylo. Finally, Wade nodded.

"Right," Death started. "Now that's all out of the way, and we all love one another again, let's watch this show and eat the fuckin' pizza."

"Show?" Kylo questioned. "Lucas, did you tell them how many *Avengers* movies there are?"

Laughing, I shook my head.

"Wait, what do you mean? How many are there?" Death asked.

"Well, if you count the movies that are connected to the Avengers, then there's many."

Death groaned. "This better be worth it."

Apparently, because Death found Black Widow hot, he didn't mind the movie at all. Wade was just happy to watch them, and me, comfortably where he could hold me and touch me whenever he wanted without hiding it.

CHAPTER EIGHTEEN
WRECK

Time fucking flew by when you were happy. I didn't realize it before Lucas, how the shit days just dragged, and you'd wish for a new one just to get over the previous one. Now, each day over the past month had passed in a flash of damn bliss because I had Lucas in my life.

However, I was starting to get sick and tired of hiding.

As I glanced around at the brothers while sitting at the bar in the compound, I wondered just how much they'd care if I was with a guy. Would they accept my happiness over the fact it was because of a dude? I hoped so because I needed them to. I wanted to stay within the club and have Lucas at my side at the same time. I knew the prez and VP would accept it, so really the others could go fuck themselves if they had a problem.

The worst one would be Saint. Not because he wouldn't like Lucas in a relationship. If anything, it would be because Lucas was with me and that I'd never been with a guy before. Saint would worry I wasn't fully in this with Lucas and just messing around, just testing the waters, but he didn't know how much I cared for Lucas.

My phone chimed. I pulled it out and smiled when I saw Lucas's name on there.

Lucas: Just picked up Mom and Dad from the airport and dropping them at our aunt's. I think Zion is heading to the compound after.

Me: What are you trying to tell me?

Lucas: Well, that you can come over... if you want to that is. You might be busy and I didn't even ask. Wait, are you working tonight and I forgot about it?

Hell, I loved his ramblings.

Me: Never busy for you. I'll be by in a couple of hours. Unless you have studying to do? You said you've got a test tomorrow.

Lucas: I do have a test, but I'm all studied out. I just want to see you.

My chest expanded.

Me: Then I'll be there.

Lucas: xoxoxo

Christ, he was a goof, but I loved him for it. He was my sanity, my calm. I couldn't see my days without him in them. Fuck me, but I was a goner for the man.

Shit... I loved him.

I fucking loved him.

Realizing it and accepting it just felt right. Over the past month, we'd got to know each other on all levels. I knew what he hated, what he liked, what made him smile, laugh, and stammer in shyness. He was also the only one who knew all of me.

One night we'd been lying in bed, and I'd told him about my shit parents. How when I'd turned eighteen, they threw me out because they were sick of taking care of me. When they'd died a year later in a car crash, I couldn't find it in me to cry. No emotion had struck me by the news because they'd treated me like I was nothing but a pain in their asses. Why they even had me in the first place, I didn't know. The one good thing about my parents giving me life was that I molded my own existence into something I was proud of. Even though I lived in the compound, I wasn't hurting for cash. Shit, I was already looking for a place that I could call home instead of a room. A place I could take Lucas to and we could be ourselves without worrying about Saint catching us. Then again, it was getting to the time Saint had to know.

"Wreck, what's happenin', brother?" Country asked as he took the stool next to me.

"Not much, Prez. Same old shit."

He tapped the bar and the prospect, or as Lucas called him, Kylo, put a beer on the counter for him. Prez took a drag and then turned to me. "Gotta say, brother, never seen you more yourself than I have in the last month. Shit, it's like a weight has been lifted off you, and you're damn happy all the time. Who has you happy?"

Fuck.

"Just someone."

"Brother, you know the club. You know that when a brother gets in close with someone, we gotta do a background check on them to see if there's anythin' in their past we need to worry about. Anythin' that can cause shit for the club. We've held off outta respect, hopin' you would come to us, but you haven't."

Fucking hell. I knew the rules, but I'd wanted to keep Lucas a secret a while longer and that really was only because of Saint.

I scrubbed a hand over my face and nodded. "You won't need a background check on this person."

He eyed me and eventually nodded. "I believe you, but I still gotta know. It's okay if you don't tell the others yet, but why all the secrecy over this?"

Leaning in, I said, "Lucas Storey." I moved back and witnessed when the name hit Country. His eyes widened, his head swung my way, and then he whistled.

"Saint's gonna kill you."

"And that's why we haven't said anythin' yet. We wanted time to ourselves, get to know one another first before the shit hit the fan."

He chuckled. "Good luck to you, brother." He held his hand out, and I shook it. He pulled me close and whispered, "Stay strong. People will give you shit, but like I said, I ain't seen you this happy in a fuckin' long time. You deserve it, no matter who you're with. Shit, I'm proud you found your fuckin' one."

I nodded, knowing I would take on the fucking world to make sure Lucas stayed at my side and in my life. He dropped my hand and patted my back.

"Baby," Isla cooed from Country's other side. Country had been seeing this younger woman for a few weeks. I wasn't sure if it would last, but he seemed happy to see her.

"Hey, darlin'," he said, curling his arm around her. "Where's your girl at?"

"She's talking with State at the other end of the bar."

We all looked down there to see State grinning down at a woman who was waving her hand around as she spoke about something. I knew that look because I'd used it the first time I'd listened to Lucas. State found her appealing. She didn't seem his usual type though. He went for tall and skinny. This woman was shorter and on the plump side.

"You want a drink?" Country asked Isla.

"No, I'm good. I'm driving tonight. It was the only way I could get Courtney here, that I promised I would drive her home, and she could have a few drinks to relax."

I stood from the stool, and Country's eye swung to me. "You jettin'?"

"Yeah, Prez. Got some place to be."

He winked. "Have fun."

I grinned because I knew I would.

It was another hour, though, before I got away since Tech came to me with a problem at Polished Pussies and Penises. I had to head over there and be backup for some other brothers since a bunch of drunk bachelor party dickheads had arrived.

By the time I got out of there, three pricks would have a few extra bruises to deal with at the wedding. One of them would be the groom, who wouldn't leave Fantasia, one of our women, alone.

It left me in a crap mood, but I knew Lucas would have me feeling better in seconds. Hell, all I had to do was see his smile, and I'd be better.

I parked my car in the driveway since Saint wouldn't be there, and Lucas would have Saint's car in the garage. Lucas didn't like to drive. He preferred to walk everywhere, but if he had to, he borrowed Saint's car. He was slowly saving up for his own.

When I reached the front door, I heard noises on the inside. Before I could unlock it, the door swung open, and in it stood Saint.

Fuck.

"Hey, brother, what are you doin' here?"

"Just dropped by to see you." As soon as it was out of my mouth, I realized it sounded lame. I only usually came over when Saint had asked because, before Lucas got there, I felt like I didn't want to intrude on Saint's time alone or with one of his many women.

"Cool, come on in. I was just runnin' out to check the car for Lucas's phone. He's freakin' out he can't find it."

"I am not. Okay, maybe a little. Hi, Wa—Wreck." He smiled as he stopped beside his brother. "I'll go and check the car. You go and see if Mom needs help in the kitchen."

"Your parents are here? Shit, brother, I'll come back when it's not family time."

"Bullshit, Wreck. Get in here." He handed the keys to Lucas, who then pushed by me, and I felt his finger graze my hand as he did. "The 'rents are just here for dinner since the aunt had her family over."

"Saint, it's family dinner, I'll see you when I see you at the compound."

"Brother, Mom always makes enough food to feed an army. Get in here to eat."

I really didn't want to meet Lucas's parents. What if they hated me?

What if they judged me to be a bad person before they found out I was with their son? Shit, I wasn't dressed for the occasion either. I had on my boots, torn jeans, a Henley, and my club vest. If I'd known I was meeting the parents, I would have worn a fucking shirt or something.

Christ, my chest felt tight.

I would walk into any trouble without a problem, but this was different. Fear had my gut twisting.

"I don't know," I said just as a short, older woman, who had Lucas's wild hair, stepped up next to Saint.

"Hello, who do we have here? My, aren't you a big boy."

"Mom," Saint started, curling his arm around her shoulders. "This is a brother of mine from the club. Name's Wreck."

"Wade, yeah, uh, call me Wade, Mrs. Storey."

Saint gave me a surprised look before he covered it with a grin. "Right."

"It's so nice to meet you, Wade. Come on in and have some dinner with us."

"Thank you for the offer, but—"

"Oh, I won't take no for an answer." She smiled.

"I found it," Lucas announced, bounding up the stairs. "It was under the car. I don't know how it got there." He looked at all of us. "What's going on?"

"We're trying to talk Wade into joining us for dinner," Mrs. Storey explained.

"That's a great idea," Lucas said. He either didn't see the panic in my eyes or chose to ignore it because he was then shoving at my back. When Saint laughed and moved himself and his mom into the house more, I glared over my shoulder at Lucas.

"I am not havin' dinner with your parents. What if they hate me?"

His hands fell away when he jerked his head back in shock, but then he smiled wide. "It's sweet you're worried, but they'll love you."

"Lucas…."

"Nope, you're coming in. Besides, I'll miss you if you leave." He pouted, and I fucking wanted to kiss him.

"Fuck. Fine," I clipped and stepped into the house.

"Who do we have here?" I heard boomed. Looking up, I saw an older version of Saint sitting in the living room chair.

"Dad, this is… um, well, he's Zion's friend from the club."

His dad stood and walked closer, holding out his hand. I took it and shook. "Nice to meet you, Mr. Storey."

"You also, son. Maybe you can tell me what goes on at a biker's club. Zion isn't forthcoming, and I've seen *Sons of Anarchy*."

I laughed. "Well, I can tell you it's nothin' like that show. It's a safe place for us to come together and hang out."

"Hmm, good answer, but I'm sure I'm missing something."

I shrugged, smiling. "I can't think of what."

"Dad, leave the guy alone. He's here to have dinner and not get questioned about anything."

Mr. Storey rolled his eyes but said, "All right, kiddo."

"I'm not a kid," Lucas grumbled under his breath.

"Lucas, honey, come set the table," Mrs. Storey called. Lucas ducked into the kitchen as Saint shot out, holding three bottles of beer. I quickly took it, unscrewed the cap and took a big gulp, hoping it'd settle my gut.

I glanced at the kitchen and watched Lucas gabbing with his mom. Both of them were the same height, and now I knew where he got it from. He laughed at something his mom said, his expression soft. A small smile tugged at my lips. I felt myself relax a little, until I looked back at Mr. Storey, and he was watching me like I was an experiment.

Shit.

What had he seen? At least he wasn't glaring at me or kicking me out. Yet.

Saint sat on the couch, and I quickly took the other spare chair. Saint and his dad went on to talk about a Yankees game, and I stared at the TV, trying to think of ways to get out of there.

"Wreck, guess who came to me last night askin' if he could join the ranks at Polished Pussies and Penises?"

"Don't have a clue, who?"

"Wait a second, what's this about penises?" Mr. Storey asked.

"That you're one," Mrs. Storey said as she placed a plate on the table.

I couldn't stop a grin from appearing. Saint just laughed aloud and slapped his thigh. "Burn, old man."

"Shut up, Zion." He glanced over to the table. "Woman, is dinner ready?"

"Don't you woman me, Gerry, and yes, it is." She took a seat as Lucas walked out of the kitchen with another plate of something and put it on the table.

"Everyone good for drinks?" Lucas asked, his eyes on me.

"I'm good." And I was, not only for a drink, but if he was close, I was more than good. I stood and went to the table as Saint and Mr. Storey did. I still felt uncomfortable, but since I was sitting across from Lucas, I knew it would help.

"Pour your beers into the glasses," Mrs. Storey said. I glanced to the others.

Mr. Storey sighed. "She has this thing about being proper at the dinner table. Just go with it or she won't shut up."

"Gerry," Mrs. Storey snapped.

"Love you, dear."

She glared and then waited until we'd all poured our beers into the waiting glasses. Then she took the bottles into the kitchen.

"She's weird sometimes," Saint muttered.

"I heard that," Mrs. Storey said with another glare when she returned, then she smiled to me. "I'm just unique in all the best ways." The other three laughed.

"Anyway," Mr. Storey started. "You going to tell me what this is about penises?" He quickly pointed at his wife. "Not a word, Lucy." She laughed as she dished up her meal.

While Saint explained, I helped myself to chicken and vegetables.

At the end, Mr. Storey nodded. "Sounds like a good plan. Business is all about adjusting with times. Good thinking."

"Thanks, Dad," Saint said and then looked at me from his spot beside Lucas. "But back to the person who I heard was lookin' at joinin'. Kylo."

Lucas coughed, food dropped out of his mouth, and Mrs. Storey patted him on the back. "Swallow or spit, Lucas."

"That's what he said," Saint chimed in.

Now it was my turn to choke as a piece of meat lodged in my throat.

"Zion, your brother's choking. It's no time for that." She looked at me. "Honey, are you all right?" I nodded. "Lucas?"

"I'm okay," Lucas said hoarsely. He whacked his chest. "I'm good… just shocked. Kylo's a friend of mine, and I didn't realize he was thinking of joining."

"Joining how?" Mrs. Storey asked.

Mr. Storey snorted and shook his head. "Sweetheart, he's joining to have sex with men and women."

"Oh." Her eyes widened. "*Oh*." She ate some food as we all stared at her. I wasn't sure why the others were, but I was just surprised she was okay with all this talk. She glanced around at us. "What?"

"Where did your head go?" Mr. Storey asked.

She rolled her eyes.

"Mom's an author, and sometimes when people say things, she runs off in her head and thinks of a storyline or something," Lucas explained.

"Well, I wasn't thinking of a story. I just thought that Lucas could maybe teach him a few things with the guys if he's not experienced. You never know, you two could be more than just friends one day."

That was when something broke. Mrs. Storey gasped. "Wade, are you okay?"

"Huh?" I blinked, my sudden anger swept aside for confusion.

"Your hand," Lucas said.

I glanced down to see I'd held my glass too tight, and it had shattered. "Yeah, I'm fine. Sorry, Mrs. Storey. I'll get something to clean this up."

"Call me Lucy, honey, and call Gerry, Gerry."

I nodded, stood from the table, and happened to glance at Gerry. He was studying me with a lot of concentration.

Fuck.

I quickly stood and said, "I'll help you clean your hand." I didn't like the way Dad looked at Wade. Like he was under the microscope, and he had him all figured out. I had an idea that Dad knew Wade and I were seeing each other. What didn't help was that Wade had broken his glass from Mom's suggestion of me teaching Kylo a few things.

In the kitchen, and since we didn't have an ounce of privacy, I grabbed out the first aid kit and got as close as I could to Wade.

"Give me your hand," I told him.

He did, and as I picked out the glass, he dipped his head to whisper, "I think your dad knows about us."

Glancing back to the table, I saw Dad still watching us with a smile on his face. Thankfully Mom asked him something, and he looked away. I nodded, whispering, "I think you're right." I shrugged. "At least he seems okay by it."

Wade made a noise in the back of his throat. "He could be just waitin' for me to be alone and then bam, he'll go all papa bear on me and tell me to leave you the fuck alone," he said in a low, gruff tone, all full of worry.

I held his hand in both of mine and smiled up at him. "Relax, okay. He won't go all papa bear on you, and if he does, which I doubt it, I'll make sure to be at your side to have your back."

"I appreciate it, but what happens if he tells Saint?"

I shrugged again as I applied antiseptic cream. "Then he tells my brother, and Zion will have to learn to deal with it."

Wade's head jerked back. "You're okay with Saint findin' out?"

"Well, yes," I told him as I wrapped his hand in a bandage. He hadn't really needed one, but it kept us in the kitchen for a while longer.

"Thank fuck. I'm tired of hidin' this."

It was my turn to jerk my head back in shock. "You are?"

"Hell yes."

"So… you're okay if, um, people… I mean, your brothers know?"

Wade grinned. "Babe, I've been wantin' to tell people for a couple of weeks. I don't give a fuck who knows you're mine."

I didn't know what he said after babe.

He'd called me babe.

An endearment for lovers and partners.

"Did I lose you?" he asked, smirking. He knew what he'd done to me, made me all melty on the inside again.

"Yes," I whispered. "I mean, no, you didn't lose me."

"I wished to Christ I could kiss you right now."

I laughed. "Then I guess Zion would find out."

He flashed his teeth in a wide smile. "Yeah, he would. But don't want to scare your mom because kissin' you would usually lead into messin' around, and a head job is outta the question right now."

"Boo," I teased. I patted his waist. "Your hand is all done. You can take the bandage off when you get to the compound. You didn't really need it, but we got to stay in here longer alone."

"What are we whispering about?" Dad asked, stopping beside us. Of course, I jumped. I hadn't heard him approach. I was lost in Wade's eyes and still on the word *babe*.

He'd called me babe. I'd never forget it. Perhaps I would mark it down on the calendar.

Wade also looked shocked when Dad appeared out of nowhere. His body tensed, his jaw clenched, and he looked a little pale.

"Nothing, Dad. We're coming out now to finish dinner."

We were, until Dad's hand landed down on our shoulders. "So," he drew out quietly, "when did this start, and why doesn't Zion know about it?"

"What start?" I asked, panicked. I was no good under the spotlight.

They both stared at me.

Dad chuckled. "Never team up with this guy in anything. He gives too much away."

Wade snorted. "I'm startin' to see that, sir."

"Pshh, not sir, just Gerry."

Wade nodded. "All right, and to be honest with you, Gerry, we've been seein' each other for a month." Wade glanced at me, smiling when he saw my wide eyes. He was just going to lay it out there. "And I can't see my days without Lucas in them."

Oh my God, that was the sweetest thing ever.

"Wade," I whispered.

Dad patted Wade's shoulder. "I can see that, son. Every time you look at my boy, you're all starry-eyed. The others haven't noticed. They don't have my brains like Lucas does, but I know them, and they won't like being kept in the dark. Especially Zion."

"Dad, we wanted to get to know each other before Zion found out. We're not sure he'll be happy with it."

He studied me and nodded.

"But we also think it's time he knows," Wade added, and I nodded.

"Then, let's do it," Dad stated.

"Wait, what?" Wade said.

"We didn't mean this second," I told him.

He patted our shoulders and smiled. "No time like the present. Then at least I'm here to stop Zion killing anyone."

"Maybe I should ring in some brothers, in case," Wade suggested.

Dad laughed, then turned and went back to the table.

"What was that about?" Mom asked.

Before Dad could say anything, I grabbed Wade's wrist and pulled him toward the table. "About me. All me, I, um… you see…." I lost my courage and couldn't get the words out because Mom and Zion were staring at me.

Wade's heat hit my back. He tugged his wrist free and placed his hands on my shoulders.

I took a deep breath. "I'm dating someone and have been for the last month," I blurted.

Zion laughed. "Are you talkin' about that Gregory guy? I thought you and he were kaput ages ago."

I shook my head. "No, not him."

Zion's head tilted to the side, and he glanced from me to over my shoulder, back to me and then over again. His jaw clenched. Slowly, he pushed his chair back and stood.

Wade moved to step in front of me.

"You," Zion snarled, and I heard Mom gasp, maybe even clap, but I wouldn't look away from Wade and my brother in case I needed to kick some butt.

"Yes," Wade answered in a rough tone.

Zion faced Wade, and out of the corner of my eye, I saw Dad stand back up and come around behind my brother.

"You came to *my* house, seduced *my* brother, and now you two are datin'?"

Wade nodded once. "Sounds about right."

"You've never fuckin' been with a guy, and you pick my brother to test this shit out?"

"Zion, language," Mom tried.

"Fuck the language. Who the fuck do you think you are, Wreck? You do not get to play my brother and then crush him when you walk away after a taste."

"Zion, calm down," Dad suggested.

"I won't walk away from him," Wade stated harshly. "You can think what you want, but I know what Lucas and I have is real."

"Real bullshit is what I call it," Zion clipped. He took a step closer.

"Zion, don't, we're happy," I inserted as I moved beside Wade. Only Wade wouldn't have it. He reached out and gently pushed me back behind him.

Zion's eyes narrowed more. "You think I would hurt my brother?"

"No. Never. But I know you're thinkin' about punchin' me, and I won't have Lucas hurt in the process."

"Oh, wow," Mom muttered. "Zion, sit down."

"No, Mom." He waved a hand toward us. "He's just playin' some sick game with Lucas. I won't fuckin' have it. You two are breakin' up."

"You're being stupid, Zion," I told him.

"I'm not. He's been straight all his fuckin' life, and now he's changin'? Christ, I don't even know why, but he ain't doin' it with my brother."

Wade dropped his head, and when he spoke, it was in an icy tone. "You know me, brother. You fuckin' know me." He looked up. "When was the last time you saw me this happy?"

Zion opened his mouth, closed it, and blinked.

"Exactly. I've never been happy, and I didn't know what was missin' until I met your brother. Jesus, Lucas brings peace inside me, and I won't give that up for anythin' or anyone. I don't know how long this'll last, but I'm goddamn prayin' it'll be for-fuckin'-ever. You're askin' me to give up this? I won't do it. Lucas is mine."

I heard a sniffle, but I watched Zion as he ground his teeth together and fisted his hands.

"You're a motherfuckin' prick for doin' this. You should have come to me first before even chasin' Lucas."

"You would have said no," Wade told him, which was true.

Zion shifted his eyes to me, where I peeked over Wade's shoulder. "You want this fucker?"

I nodded. "Yes."

"Even though he's never been with a guy before and this could all just be a phase?"

"Yes," I said again. "It'll always be yes because he does make me happy. Not only that, I know I'll always be protected as well."

My brother looked between us, and then quickly, he punched Wade in the face.

"Zion," I yelled, and grabbed Wade as he straightened. I ran my hands over his face; a mark was already showing on his jaw. What was weird was that Wade was smiling. "What are you grinning about?" I demanded. Had he lost his mind?

Zion snorted. "Because he knows I'll accept it as long as the fucker doesn't hurt you. That was me givin' my consent, but also a fuck you for keepin' it from me."

My heart pounded in my chest.

Had my brother really accepted this?

"So, you're not going to be an idiot about this?" I asked, needing confirmation.

"Lucas, you're the smarter one out of us, and if you want to tie yourself to this fool, then… now that it's processed in my head, I'm not gonna stop this."

A smile grew on my lips. "Really?"

Zion rolled his eyes and then turned to go sit back down. Dad was also returning to his seat.

I glanced up at Wade, who was grinning down at me. "You happy?" he asked.

"More than happy, whatever that is," I answered just as he cupped my cheeks and dipped down to give me a kiss.

"Jesus, I only gave my consent. Doesn't mean you need to suck his face off in front of me."

Chuckling, Wade straightened and curled an arm around my shoulders. "You'll get used to it," he told Zion.

"I think it's sweet," Mom cooed. She stood and came at us with open arms. "This is amazing. Welcome to the family, Wade." She hugged us tightly together.

"I'm surprised you two didn't see it from a mile away like I did," Dad said, sitting back and taking a sip of his beer, acting like a know-it-all.

"What are you talking about?" Mom asked while we all sat back down, only I moved around to sit beside Wade.

"As soon as I met the guy, I knew something was going on between those two. It's all in the eyes."

Zion scratched his nose with his middle finger. "Whatever, old man. I've been too busy to notice anything." Zion looked to Wade. "Anyone else know?"

"West and Kylo," I said.

"Country and Death. Country because he's prez, and Death because he noticed some things as well."

"What the fuck did I miss? Christ, I feel like I've been blind."

"Anyway," Dad started, and all of a sudden, I got scared because he was looking at Wade. "Tell us a bit about yourself, Wade, since you're dating our son."

"Dad, no," I said.

Zion rubbed his hands together and grinned evilly. "Yes."

Mom waved her hand in front of her. "Wait, I have a question. As Zion pointed out before, Wade, you've slept with a lot of women. Did you practice safe sex?"

"Mom!" I cried.

Dad groaned. "Dear God, Lucy."

Zion just laughed his butt off and pointed at Mom. "Good one."

I grabbed Wade's hand under the table and gave it a squeeze. "Please excuse my strange and very intrusive family. You don't have to answer anything you don't want to."

Wade leaned back in his seat and smirked. "It's all right." I went to say something, but then his hand landed on the back of my neck, and he rubbed there. I blinked and got distracted from his touch.

Wade kept his hand there and said, "I've always practiced safe sex. I was born into a family who never really wanted a kid, so I made sure to not have a kid with someone who would have been just a one-night hookup."

Everyone stared at him.

He shrugged. "Just keepin' it real. My parents didn't care what I did, if I was fed, or where I was. When I hit eighteen, I got out. I found a place, a club of great men who became my family. They taught me more about life than my parents ever had. A year later, my parents died in a car crash. I can't say I was broken up about it because I wasn't."

"Of course you weren't," Mom said. "And if they were still around, I would be on their front step, cursing them black and blue for doing such a thing."

Wade tensed beside me, surprised by Mom's outburst. He cleared his throat. "Ah, thanks." Mom smiled warmly at him. His hand tightened on my neck.

"What do you do with your days now?" Dad asked.

"I'm part owner of the Polished Pussy clubs. I assist there on a rotating roster with Saint, Country, and State."

Zion snorted. "We manage the shit outta that club with a couple of assistant managers when we're not in, like now. And then, with the other two startin' to take off, we're run off our feet so we'll have to look at hirin' more managers. Plus, with the changes we're makin', the money will be rollin' in."

Suddenly, Wade blurted, "I'm lookin' at gettin' my own place soon. Right now, I live at the compound, but I want a place to call my own. Somewhere Lucas will feel comfortable to be, and it'll be in a safer area."

My heart felt like it was pumping so hard to get out of my chest and jump out at Wade to curl up in a purring heap in his lap.

I dropped my fork and turned to him.

"Shit, we're about to see more PDA. Mom, get a gag bag ready for me."

"Shut it, Zion," Mom said, and her voice sounded like she was on the verge of tears.

"You are?" I asked Wade softly.

"Yeah, babe. Can't live in the compound forever." His hand left my neck to tuck some hair behind my ear, then he placed it back. He was grinning at me and I wanted to kiss him so much.

Dang it all.

Wade met me halfway and right there in front of my parents, we shared a sweet, soft kiss. We only pulled away when Zion started gagging.

Still having his gaze, I told him, "You know I'm not happy because you're getting a house, right? I don't want you to think that. I just think it's the sweetest thing ever that you thought of me with the choices you made."

"We're together, yeah?"

"Well, yes." I nodded.

He tipped his chin up at me, as if that was answer enough. Then he added, "At least then I'll know you'll be there safe, under the alarm system, so you can study and I won't have to worry you're surrounded by fuckheads who'll take advantage of you when you're in a zone."

Zion snorted, then laughed with Dad.

Mom, who was smiling like a madwoman, said, "He really does go into a zone."

Wade sighed. "He does. Totally oblivious to what's around him. You can't do that at the compound. I've already heard the brothers sayin' how good-lookin' you are. I do not share."

"They have?"

"That's what you pick to say?" Wade growled.

"Um, no, I'm only worried about a certain man thinking I'm good-looking." I scoffed. "Who cares about the others."

He tugged me in, kissed me hard and quickly, and then said, "Exactly."

CHAPTER TWENTY
WRECK

By the time dinner finished and all questions were out of the way, we stood at the front door saying goodbye to Lucas's parents. For now. Apparently, they wanted to get to know me because Lucy said she could see good things for Lucas and me. Hell, my chest puffed out at the comment because it sounded like she accepted me being with her son.

Saint was driving them over to their aunt's place. I'd already moved my bike and after Lucy gave out hugs, and Gerry handshakes, they were in the car waiting on Saint.

"I'm headin' to the compound after," he said.

I curled Lucas into my side with an arm around his shoulders. "If you could not talk about this to the brothers, it'd be appreciated. I'll be bringin' it up at the next church."

He eyed us just as Lucas wrapped his arms around my middle. He sighed. "Fine." He started for the car in the garage. "Oh, and keep your naked bits to the bedroom."

"Unfair," Lucas called. "I still have nightmares about you doing women over furniture."

Saint chuckled. "Good times. But seriously, this is my house. No fuckin' in the livin' room or kitchen."

"We haven't even done that," Lucas blurted and then buried his head into my chest from embarrassment. He missed Saint stumbling forward. He spun back with wide eyes and stared at me.

"Holy fuck, you really do care," he stated.

I nodded.

He gave me a salute. "Respect, brother. Respect." As soon as he disappeared into the garage, I guided Lucas back into the house and locked the door behind us.

"You want dessert?" I asked, with a quirk of an eyebrow. I thinned my lips to stop from grinning when Lucas blushed. "Babe, I'm talkin' about ice cream." I pulled him to the couch and sat on it, maneuvering him onto my lap easily because he was tiny. Just the right size for me though. "I remember someone eatin' outta the container when I walked into the house."

He rolled his eyes. "That wasn't a good night…. Well, it ended up being, but when you saw me, I was devastated you were with a woman."

"Devastated?" I questioned.

"Completely."

Lucas bit his bottom lip when I ran my hands up and down his waist. "Hmm, sounds like I have to make it up to you."

He shook his head. "Nope, you already did when you kissed me that night."

"Really?"

He nodded, and I tugged him forward so he could feel my hard-on. He gasped and smiled softly. When he rocked against me, I groaned.

"Then you let me know if there's anythin' else I can do for you," I told him against his neck before I bit there.

"Oh… um, you were talking about dessert before."

I ran my tongue up the side of his neck and sucked in his earlobe. Once again, he rocked against me, his breathing erratic. "I was," I said. "Have you thought of somethin'?"

"Y-Yes," he whispered, and my cock jerked. I glided my hands up and under his tee, running my thumbs over and around his taut nipples.

"What's that, babe?"

He moaned and ground down over me again. I gripped his hips to stop him, or I'd be coming in my jeans. Christ, my guy's body, his words, his voice, everything about him made me crazy.

"I… I love it when you call me that," he admitted. When I saw his eyes glaze, I knew he had. His body relaxed, the pulse in his neck beating hard. I liked giving it to him, liked getting any reaction out of him.

"Babe," I muttered against his neck. He rocked down, at least tried, but I had a hold of him. "What dessert are you after?"

"You. Just you."

He gasped when I gripped his ass and picked him up as I stood. He clung to me, kissing my neck, my jaw, and cheek as I walked us down the hall and into his room.

As soon as we were through the door, I placed Lucas on his feet and swept his tee off, throwing it to the floor. I removed my vest while Lucas eagerly undid my jeans button. I put my vest on the back of the chair and tugged my own T-shirt off, dropping it to the ground. Lucas unzipped my jeans and then worked on his own.

I leaned in and captured his lips, cupping the back of his head. Using my free hand, I pushed his jeans down his legs. I felt him kick them off, and then his hands were at my waist, shoving my jeans down. Only they got stuck on my boots.

"Fuck," I clipped. I pulled away to kick off my boots and then fling my jeans and boxers off with them. Lucas removed his socks, and we were back to kissing and touching each other, anywhere we wanted.

Reaching between us, I took hold of both our cocks and slid my palm over them together. The kiss stopped. Lucas panted out his breaths while he rested his head against my chest to watch my hand work us.

"Goddamn, this feels good," I told him, because it did. He hummed under his breath.

We'd been messing around for the last month, trying different ways to get each other off without actually doing it. I'd fucking loved each and every moment. It always got me off. *He* always got me off. I fucking loved his body, his flat chest, his cock, his ass. Especially when, a couple of nights ago, I had my fingers in his warm, tight hole. He'd gone crazy, moaning, crying my name, and I'd come in my jeans again because he'd been rocking over my erection.

He was the sexiest person I'd ever had.

And he was mine.

All damn mine.

Hell, I couldn't be happier.

"Stop," Lucas whispered, his hand going over mine around both of us.

"What's wrong?" I asked.

He lifted his head, his eyes full of desire and something else I couldn't put my finger on. He licked his lips. "I want…." He glanced to the side.

I gripped his waist and asked, "What do you want, babe?"

"More."

"In what way?" I questioned. I was guessing he wanted to go all the way, and hell I wanted it as well, but I needed him to be sure and for Lucas to actually tell me.

His cheeks pinked. I gently pinched his chin and brought his gaze back to mine. "Tell me," I ordered.

He scraped his top teeth over his bottom lip. Then he whispered words that had my cock throbbing and leaking in eagerness. "I want to feel you inside me."

Fuck me.

"Yeah?"

He nodded. "Yes."

"Get on the bed, Lucas," I ordered, my voice thick and rough.

He tried to hide his smile with his hand, but I caught it. He liked getting what he wanted and hell, I would give him anything in my power.

Lucas slowly walked over to the bed, climbed on it, and then rolled over to his back. His hair splayed out on the pillow. His full lips looked redder than usual from all the kissing. His cock was hard and ready for its release.

Stunning.

There was no way I could touch myself right then or else I'd be embarrassing myself. Instead, I asked, "Where's the lube, condom?"

He rolled to the side, to his bedside table. He pulled it open quickly, but too fast because the whole thing came open and dropped to the floor. He flushed but grabbed the items and set them on the bed. Grinning, I took the steps to the end of the bed.

"Tell me what way would be better for you."

He blew out a breath and shrugged. "Any, I'll… um." He glanced around the room.

"Babe," I said, and his eyes shot back to me. "It's just you and me in here, say anythin' you want. You got nothin' to be embarrassed about. Nothin'."

"Okay," he whispered. "It will probably be best with you on top or, um, me on my knees and you behind me. But I'll, ah, need prep first."

Fuck me. His words pounded into my cock.

"Spread 'em for me, babe," I ordered.

"Wade," he said softly.

"Babe," I replied and quirked my eyebrow.

He grumbled something under his breath, probably giving himself a pep talk about how he shouldn't feel embarrassed about showing me all of him. He would eventually understand. He would eventually give me what I wanted without complaint because he would know he would benefit from it in the end also.

Only this time, I would help him.

I kneeled on the bed at the end. Lucas watched as I slowly

reached out for his ankles. For a while, I rubbed my hands up and down his shins, then gripped his ankles and separated his legs. I moved them up, so his knees bent, and I could get a better look at the spot where I wanted to be.

I loved how smooth his ass was. I shifted forward to lie between his legs. I glanced up to him and found he'd covered his face with his hands.

"Lucas," I clipped.

He didn't say or do anything.

"Babe," I tried again, softer.

"I-If you, um, keep going, I won't feel so, ah, bad… if that makes sense?"

It did. He needed touch and sensation to take him away from what his brain was saying to him. I grabbed the tube of lube, opened it, and squeezed some on my fingers before dropping it to the bed. Leaning in, I kissed the side of his inner thigh, and his body jolted from the contact. I trailed my tongue up until I leaned up and sucked the tip of his cock into my mouth.

He moaned. His hands moved from his face and gripped the blankets under us. As I licked and sucked, I gently reached out and rubbed my slicked fingers over his hole.

He rocked up into my mouth. "Wade," he cried. I circled around his hole, making it wet, before slowly inserting one finger. "Oh, oh, yes," he chanted.

Fuck me, but he was tight. Nothing like I'd felt before and my dick wanted in.

Lifting my mouth off his dick, I watched as I pushed in further, searching for the nub I knew would be there, and that would—"Hell," Lucas cried, as soon as I touched his prostate. He dug his feet into the bed and ground down on my finger, but I was already pulling it back out and gliding it on the outer edge again. He whimpered, wanting more, but he would have to be patient. I didn't want to hurt him.

"Wade," he pleaded.

"I've got you," I answered, and pushed my finger back in with another. He gasped, arching back. When I ran over the right area again, he moaned loud and long.

"Wade, honey, please," he begged.

Jesus Christ, he was making my own patience run low. Sweat beaded over my brow. I wiped it with the back of my free arm before sliding it under his ass and taking a handful. Leaning in, I kissed Lucas's thigh and nipped at his skin.

"Please, Wade, please, want you."

Fucking hell.

"Where do you want me, babe?" I growled as I scissored my fingers, stretching him enough for me, at least I hoped, but I doubted because he was damn tight.

"Inside me," he said, lifting his head to look down at me between his legs. He licked his lips and panted out his breaths. "Please."

"Babe, maybe we should just keep doin' this. You're tight. I don't wanna hurt you."

He shook his head and clenched his jaw when my finger ran over the right area inside of him.

"No, can't wait, won't wait. Wade, need you."

Fuck me, how was I supposed to resist that? I couldn't, not when he was so needy for my dick. For me.

Withdrawing my fingers, I got to my knees, and Lucas watched with hooded eyes as I grabbed the condom, ripped it open, and rolled it on. When Lucas started running his hand up and down his stomach and chest, I ground my teeth together and tugged my balls back down. I grabbed the lube and slathered it over my hard-on. Lucas's hand dipped, and he slid his palm up and down his dick. I quickly slapped it away.

"If you do that, I won't fuckin' last. I'm already on edge from watchin' you just take my fingers."

His smile was sweet. "Then you better hurry before I lose it myself from knowing you're here, mine, and how you're about to be inside me."

I closed my eyes and tugged my balls once again. Opening my eyes, I glared down at him. "No talkin'."

His eyes brightened as he laughed. "Okay," he whispered, amusement in his eyes.

"Lucas," I warned as I applied more lube to and around his hole. Of course, I couldn't resist slipping a finger in and watching him gasp, arch, and close his eyes. When I took it out, he opened his lids and glared.

"Come here, Wade," he ordered.

It was fucking cute.

I pressed my hands onto the bed and leaned forward, dipping low so I could kiss him. He wrapped me up and gave back as good as he got. I glided my lips down to his ear and sucked on his lobe. My Lucas was back to breathing hard.

"Lift your legs up, babe. Onto my shoulders."

Gone were the actions of shyness. He lifted them and bared his hole to me, ready for fucking. Reaching between us, I lined up my cock to his hole and slowly pushed forward.

"Wade," he said softly.

"Tell me if it's too much. Tell me if you hurt, babe."

He nodded, reaching up to cup my cheeks. "I'll let you know."

"Good," I grunted and pushed in a little more.

I locked my jaw tight and closed my eyes. His tightness surrounded me so fucking snugly it wasn't funny because already, I was on the verge of losing my load.

His hands gripped my forearms, and I opened my eyes to see him flinch. I started to pull out, but his hands moved to my hips, and he said, "No, just wait a moment." I shook my head. "Please. I need to adjust, and then it'll be good. I'll be good."

Christ, I hated the fact he was uncomfortable, but I'd said it to myself before, and I'd say it again, I'd give him anything he asked for... within reason.

I waited. My body tensed, and I wanted to push all the way in to feel him wrapped around me, but I wouldn't do that. More sweat pooled over my brow and lower back. The tip of my cock was singing its praise at the tight heat. It didn't want out. It wanted to blow into the hole, but I thought of everything else to keep the lid on it.

"All right," Lucas said. His grip on my hips hardened, and he pulled me forward, my dick sliding in more.

Fucking hell. Fucking motherfucking hell. He was perfect. He felt amazing.

"Christ, babe, you feel so damn good," I told him just as the last inch of my dick entered, and Lucas moaned. I pulled back out slowly and then in.

"Wade, God, it… it's amazing," he muttered. "More."

I withdrew from the warmth and how his body caressed mine, and then thrust back in, which caused Lucas to cry out and arch. I stilled, in case I hurt him.

"More," he demanded, opening his eyes and reaching up for me. He tugged me down, his legs dropping from my shoulders and sliding around my waist. His arms wound around my back and shoulders. With his chin tipped back, he pecked at my lips. "Fuck me, Wade," he whispered.

I groaned, slid my hands under his ass, and held on as I drew out and thrust back in. "Fuck," I clipped. "So good. Jesus, too good."

"Faster, please."

As soon as those words left Lucas's mouth, I did as asked and pumped in and out of him in a frenzy of wild fucking.

"Wade," he panted. "I'm close."

Christ, he wasn't even touching himself. "Me too, babe, fuck, me too."

Lucas's arms pressed harder around me, his thighs squeezing me, and I could feel his feet digging into the bed as I kept fucking him over and over.

"Wade," he cried and then moaned, just before I felt his load wet us between our stomachs. He came, causing his ass to tighten even more around me, and then I was lost. I groaned and cursed through my own release as I emptied inside him.

I rested for a moment on top of him, but I didn't want to squish him with all my weight. I pulled my cock free, even when I didn't want to, and moved to his side, curling him into my body with an arm under his head and one over his slick waist. I didn't give a fuck we were getting his load everywhere. I just wanted to goddamn hold him.

He ran his hand up and down my arm. He hummed under his breath and said, "That was good."

I kissed his temple, his cheeks, and then adjusted my body so I could have his mouth. "That was fuckin' unreal."

A stunningly wide smile curved his lips. "It was."

"I'll get a cloth to clean you up. You stay there," I told him and slid from the bed. I nearly swayed on my damn feet after coming so fucking hard.

Lucas chuckled. "You okay?"

"Better than okay," I said, and walked from the room. I shook my head and couldn't wipe the smile from my face. He was damn perfect for me. Christ, I was already growing half hard from just thinking about being inside him. I couldn't wait to do it again, and again, for the rest of our damn lives.

After warming the washcloth, I walked back into the bedroom to find him exactly as I'd left him, with him smiling at me. He brushed some hair from his face, and I sat on the bed, first cleaning him off and then myself before dropping it to the floor.

"You sore?" I asked, getting back in the bed and dragging him close once more.

"A little. But I'm already looking forward to doing it again," he admitted before he ducked his head into my chest, embarrassed by his words. I grinned. He'd eventually learn he didn't have to be embarrassed. However, until then, I fucking liked seeing him this way as well.

Chuckling, I said, "That's good. I know I'm already lookin' forward to it."

And many more days spent with him. Hell, they didn't even have to be spent fucking. I wanted him in all ways. To talk to, to hold, to know everything about, to even fucking hold his hand. I wanted him in every way.

He was mine, and soon, everyone would know, and I didn't give a shit because it meant I could do all those things without hiding. Except the fucking. That'd be behind closed doors. No one got to see Lucas as he came.

"You make me happy, Lucas."

He lifted his head and smiled softly. "You make me happy, Wade."

I tucked some of his wild hair behind his ear. "Thank you for the second chance."

He shook his head. "Thank you for wanting me."

"Always will."

He kissed my jaw. "Same."

CHAPTER TWENTY-ONE
LUCAS

It had been a month since Wade and I had first had sex. He'd made me wait for a few days before he got to do it again because he wanted to make sure I wouldn't be sore for the second time. I'd told him my body would get used to it, but he wouldn't listen. It had been our first argument.

Standing in the bedroom with my hands on my hips, I shouted, "Don't you think I know my body just a bit more than you?"

"No."

I growled under my breath. "You're being stubborn, Wade Williams."

"Usin' the full name. At least I know what to look out for when you're pissed at me. But I'm not givin' up on this, Lucas. We wait."

I threw my hands out, then planted them back on my hips. "I'm fine," I snarled. "I know I'm fine. I was fine the next dang day."

He stood from the bed and stomped across the room to me. He cupped my cheek and lifted my angry gaze to his. "You may feel fine, but I won't risk it. I didn't like you feelin' uncomfortable the first time. I don't like the thought of you in pain. Your ass is sensitive. You admitted it just this damn mornin'. For my sake, please give in on this, and I'll suck you off."

I went to argue back until the last words registered. "Well, okay then," I replied.

His grin was smug. He'd won, but in the end, I did too because I came, and okay, he did as well, but still, I felt like I won.

Since then, we were at it like rabbits. He couldn't get enough of me, like I couldn't him. I'd also been right. My body may need a day of recuperation, depending on how hard he'd taken me, but my body adjusted to him.

The only nights we slept apart from one another were when he was working, which was three times a week, or if I studied and stayed up late in the living room so he could catch up on some sleep.

"Morning" came grumbled from behind me. Wade and his grumpy self had just woken.

I glanced over my shoulder from the stove and smiled. "Morning back. There's coffee in the pot that's ready for you." Wade had brought a coffee maker since he didn't like instant, and he was here all the time.

Instead of getting the coffee, he came up behind me and kissed my shoulder. Topless, his skin warmed mine. "What're you makin'?"

"Pancakes." I turned my head enough for him to give me what I wanted: a quick kiss before I faced the pan, so I didn't burn them.

"I'm gonna get fat eatin' your cookin'," he said, his voice low and gruff from sleep still.

I laughed. "I doubt it. You work out every day. Besides, my not-so-healthy cooking goes hand in hand with your healthy stuff."

His hands slid around to my naked stomach, and he tugged me back so I could feel his erection. "We fit together well then."

"We do." I grinned. He glided a hand down and into my sweatpants, where he wound it around my thickened length. He ran it up and down, getting me harder than I already was.

A throat cleared. "Please tell me you're not jerkin' my brother off in my kitchen."

Wade chuckled, but he didn't let go of me. "All right, I won't tell you that."

"Brother, get your fuckin' hand outta there."

Wade kissed my neck again and removed his hand, turning toward Zion. "You gonna make me a coffee?"

"Get your own," Zion said. "You practically live here. I ain't waitin' on you."

"True. But I've got another place to look at this afternoon. Hopefully it'll be the one," Wade said as he got himself a coffee, and I tried to calm my raging erection.

Wade had been to many houses, but none were what he'd been looking for. He knew what he wanted, and I knew him, which meant he'd make sure he'd get exactly that.

"How many would this be you've checked out?" Zion asked.

"This will be the fifteenth," I said for him.

Zion laughed. "Fingers crossed for you then, brother. Now, are you two comin' to the compound tonight?"

"I'll see how it goes in church this mornin'," Wade said. He hadn't told the rest of his brothers yet because I'd asked him not to. That was only because I wanted to give us a little more time to be just us without anyone else saying anything to get him riled. It had been a few weeks ago when we'd gone out on our first date, and some drunk guy had made a comment when Wade had kissed me. I was lucky Wade listened to me to leave it alone; that was after he'd given the guy a black eye. I worried he would take on his brothers if one of them made a snide comment, which was bound to happen. Some of them just learned to grow up that way. However, Wade was going to let the brothers know who he was dating before the party at the compound that night where I would go as, not Zion's brother, but Wade's partner.

"I'm sure the brothers won't care."

"We'll see, but if anyone says anythin' to Lucas tonight, I'll fuckin' have their blood."

"I'll be right there backin' you up, Wreck, you know that."

Wade grunted.

"Hell, I won't be the only one either. Don't stress over it," Zion said.

I kept quiet because I was a little worried. Not about showing I was committed to Wade, but over Wade wanting blood if they were idiots about us being together.

My phone started ringing. Wade picked mine up from the table and looked at it. "It's Mom," he said just before he answered with, "Hey, Mom, you've got Wade here." I glanced at Zion to find him smiling like I was. Mom and Dad adored Wade so much they'd told him to call them Mom and Dad. I loved they did that for him, knowing it meant a lot to him.

"Nah, he's awake and cookin' breakfast. Hang on, I'll put you on speaker."

"Morning, my boys" came through the phone.

"Morning," I replied.

"Hey, Momma Bear," Zion called.

"Lucas, good luck on your test today, and Zion, a friend of mine has a daughter who's just moved to the area—"

"No thanks, Mom. Love you, but I've gotta get a shower in before the other two hog it. Bye." He quickly raced out of the kitchen.

"Zion!" Mom yelled.

"He's gone, Mom," I said.

She sighed. "That boy, he'll never settle down and find the one like you two have."

Wade and I looked at each other and grinned. As I dished up the last of the cooked pancakes, I said, "He will, Mom. It just might take longer."

"Then I'll never get grandkids I can spoil. Unless… are you two looking at a surrogate or adopting?"

Wade choked on the sip of coffee he'd just had. I laughed. "Mom, it's too soon to even think of that."

She sighed again. "I suppose you're right."

"How's the house coming?" I asked. Mom and Dad were still living with our aunt at the moment because once they'd come back from Australia, neither wanted to leave again. Dad hadn't realized he'd missed home so much. Currently, they were building a two-bedroom house about fifteen minutes away from Zion's.

"Another couple of months and we'll be in there. It's just lucky your aunt has a big enough house for all of us until it's done."

"That is lucky," I said, aware they would have been staying here with us and sleeping in the living room.

"Anyway, I better go. Your father wants to go to the hardware store, and I have to go with him so he doesn't spend all our money on useless things."

"Good luck," Wade said.

"Thank you. Love to you both."

"Love you, Mom."

When Wade didn't respond, uncomfortable with the word and expressing his emotions because of his asshole parents, Mom called, "Wade?"

"Ah, yeah, you too."

She giggled. "That'll do." Then she hung up.

I placed the plate on the table and walked over to him, slipping my arms around his waist. "You'll get there."

"It's not because I don't want to say it. I just ain't tellin' your mom I love her when I haven't said it to you first."

My heart perked up and skipped a beat before taking off in flight, along with my stomach.

"Um… okay," I muttered.

He tucked some hair behind my ear. "Eyes, Lucas."

I looked up at him.

He smiled softly. "You know, right?"

"What?"

"That I fuckin' love you."

My stupid eyes chose that moment to water for no reason, and all my swoony emotions were swirling inside me.

I licked my lips, cleared my throat, and said, "I had a feeling you did, but hearing it makes it even better." I thumped my forehead against his chest. "I love you too."

He chuckled. "Babe, I'd like to see you when you say it so I can kiss you."

Sucking in a deep breath, I lifted my head and told him, "I love you too, Wade."

"Thank you for givin' it to me."

"Same. Except your love to me."

He grinned, then dipped down to take my mouth in a smooth, soft, passionate kiss.

I was on a high for the rest of the day from Wade telling me he loved me. I was sure I aced the test as well, but that didn't even compare to Wade's words. I had just walked into the house when my phone rang, and Wade's name showed on the screen.

"Hi," I answered.

"Hey, babe. All good for tonight, but if anyone fucks with you, I'll deal with it."

"I'm sure it will be fine."

He grunted. "We'll see. I'm just headin' out to look at this house. Want to come with me?"

"Do you have time to pick me up?" I asked. I'd been to a few houses with Wade to check them out. It didn't bother me what it was like or where it was because if Wade was there, I would be happy to spend a few nights in the week there with him.

"Always got time, babe. Trix will wait until we get there anyway."

Trix. I wasn't a fan of the realtor Wade was with. She looked at my man like he was a roller coaster, and she wanted a ride… or ten. Still, I supposed looking wasn't too bad, as long as touching never happened.

"Okay, I'd love to come."

"See you soon," he replied, and I waited for him to hang up, but he didn't.

"Wade?"

"Love you, babe."

I gripped the table in front of me as I melted. "Love you, Wade Williams."

He grunted, but it was one of his happy ones. There was something in his tone that helped me differentiate between them.

Before Wade showed, I'd managed to get in a quick bite to eat and was out in front waiting for him while I read from one of my textbooks. Since it was finals time, I had to use all the spare time I had to study.

When I heard a car pull into the drive, I looked up and smiled. Wade had his window down, and he called out, "I'm surprised you heard me. You didn't get a chance to get in your bubble, babe?"

I rolled my eyes. "No, I haven't been long out here, smartass." I put my book down and left it on the seat on the front porch. I doubted anyone would be interested in stealing it. I jumped down the stairs, nearly tripped, but straightened and went to the passenger door while my boyfriend laughed at me.

As soon as I was in the car, he cupped the back of my head and tugged me into him. "Hey." He grinned.

"Hi," I whispered, lost in his eyes. But then I closed them because his lips were on mine.

We broke apart, and Wade ordered, "Seat belt."

I snorted but did as he asked. Without a doubt, he would have sat at the front of the house until I gave in. I knew when to pick my battles.

When we drove toward the general area of the compound, I asked, "How did it really go this morning?"

His jaw clenched, which wasn't a good sign. "A couple made dickish comments, but it settled down, and as far as I know, they'll be on their best behavior. Helps I have Saint, Death, Country, and State at my back."

Reaching out, I smiled and placed my hand on his thigh, squeezing. "Even if they do something, will you try and stay calm? I don't care what they say. I've learned to ignore mean people like that."

His hand covered mine and then gripped. "That's the thing, babe. You don't have to learn to live with it. You don't put up with it, and I won't allow anyone to treat you fuckin' different."

He seemed worked up, so I said, "Okay, honey."

He relaxed a little, and we drove in silence for a while longer. My stomach churned in tension with worry about tonight, but all I could do was see how things went and then deal with it when the time came.

"There's somethin' I gotta tell you," he said.

Facing him, my stomach tightened, and I replied, "Yes?"

"Death looked into that asshole's problem with his father." Mitch. "On the news tonight, there'll be an announcement of fuckface's dad being sent to jail for drug trafficking."

I gasped. "What? Did he actually deal in drugs?"

"No, but Death set it up to make sure it looked like it. No one will find fault in Death's proof over him, which was sent in anonymously."

"Wow. Um, okay. That's good then, yes?"

"Yeah, babe. It's good because the father deserves every year he gets in jail."

"Then I'm glad it got sorted." It also showed me just how much the club could do and would do for someone in a difficult situation. Even after Mitch was a dickhead to me, he didn't deserve what his father put him and his mother through. "You guys are amazing, you know that, right?"

His eyes were warm went they slid to me before moving back to the road. "Makes me damn happy to have your support."

"You always will. So will the club. I now understand you all deal with things in your own way. In the right way, even when sometimes it's not pleasant."

His hand shot out. He hooked it behind my neck and dragged me in for a quick, hard kiss. "Wade, watch the road."

He chuckled but sat back and continued driving with his hand in mine.

When we pulled up to a two-story light gray house, I thinned my lips to keep myself from gasping. It was stunning. There was a balcony on the second level, and across the road was government land that held a mini man-made lake.

I glanced at Wade to see him taking it in. His face wasn't pinched in disgust, a good sign.

"What do you think?" he asked.

I shrugged. "It's completely up to you and what you think," I told him, and then quickly got out of the car so he didn't see how I was falling for it just from the first view.

Hand in hand, Wade walked with me to the front door. As we got close, it opened, and there stood the black-haired beauty, Trix.

Her eyes ran over Wade, and she didn't even glance in my direction. Like the other times, I didn't exist, even though I was holding Wade's hand.

"Wreck, so lovely to see you again." She smiled, her hand coming out for him to shake.

It was the first time I did it, but I got to her hand and shook it first. "Hi there, Trix. Remember me? I'm Lucas." Using her hand, I steered her around and back into the house. "The place is big. Don't you think, honey?"

I glanced over my shoulder to see Wade trying to fight from laughing. He smirked and said, "Yeah, babe. It's big."

I dropped Trix's hand and went back over to Wade. I hooked my hand around his arm and asked, "Do you mind if we take a look on our own?"

She lifted her gaze from my hand to me. "No, of course not. Please take your time."

"Thank you." I smiled and then led Wade away from her.

Wade leaned in and said, with humor in his voice, "Good to see you jealous, babe, but no one does it for me except you."

"Good, well, let's keep it that way."

He chuckled, saying, "Will do."

When we'd finished going through the four bedrooms, two

living rooms, three bathrooms, and the massive kitchen, I could tell Wade liked the place.

"What are you going to do?" I asked.

"Put in an offer," he said as we made our way back to Trix.

"It's not too big just for you?" I queried, because if it was only me, I would second-guess my choice.

Wade stopped. He pushed me up against the wall and placed his hands on each side of my head. "It won't be just for me. You'll be here. Want you movin' in once everythin' is done, Lucas." My body hummed, my heart hammered, and I couldn't seem to get enough oxygen in. Then he went on, "I don't want to come home to a house without you in it." He pressed a kiss to my temple. "Might be too soon to talk about it, but you need to know you're in my future, and one day, way down the track, this house won't be too big. It'll be just right because there'll be more than just the two of us. You want that, yeah?" He pulled back to search my face.

I opened my mouth and managed a squeak. Wade grinned. I cleared my throat. "I, um, yeah, I would like to work toward that."

"Then we'll do it." He growled the words before he kissed me.

CHAPTER TWENTY-TWO
WRECK

I could tell Lucas was shitting bricks as we drove toward the compound. He wouldn't be worried about himself. He was selfless like that. He'd be concerned for me and if I got into it with my brothers over us. I'd try my damn best that nothing happened tonight. I wanted it to be a good night, but if anyone was stupid enough to say stuff, then I'd stand up for the both of us.

"Do you think the owners will take my offer?" I asked as we drew closer, wanting him to relax before we arrived. Which would probably be useless.

Lucas snorted. "They would be silly not to. You're offering exactly what they're after. Unless they want to be greedy. If they try it, maybe you should find somewhere else."

"They better fuckin' not be. I want that for us. It's close to here, close to your 'rents, your college, and not far from Saint's. Added bonus, we have three hospitals in a good distance for you to try and get into."

He took my hand. "Are you sure it's what you want? You're not just looking for me, are you?"

"Fuck no. I want it, and I'm glad you like it."

"I do… um, can I say something though?"

I gave his hand a squeeze. "You don't need to ask if you can say it, just say it, babe."

"Okay," he whispered, and my dick gave a jerk behind my jeans. "Ah, you know how you asked me to move in?" I nodded. "Well, I want to help contribute to the mortgage and utilities."

"No," I stated.

"Wade…."

"No," I said again as we pulled into the compound parking lot. I shot a wave to Torch, who was manning the gate with a few other brothers.

"Wade, you're being ridiculous. Is this relationship equal, or do you think you're in charge?"

I parked the car, switched it off, and turned to him. "Babe. We're equal. I'm not sayin' you won't help, but I'd like to suggest you wait until you're workin' in a hospital. You've got a lotta shit goin' on right now, and I don't want you stressed you have to work in that café job while tryin' to study." I shrugged.

His nose was scrunched up. He hated it when I made sense but didn't want to admit it. He sighed. "Fine, but when I'm raking in the money, I want to pay however many years you have on your own."

I cupped the back of his neck. If this was what he needed to make sure he felt like it'd be our house and not just mine, then I'd give it to him. "Deal," I said, and then kissed him.

His arms wrapped around me for a second, and then he was pushing me back. "I can't go in there looking like we've just been making out in the car."

"Why the fuck not?"

"Um… some… I mean, I guess not all the brothers will like you being with a guy. It's not good to rub it in their faces."

"Babe. We're in a car, it's dark out, and I really don't give a fuck who cares about us kissin'. If you have an urge to kiss me, I want you to do it wherever and whenever you want. I'm not ashamed of us, and you shouldn't be either. Fuck 'em."

His eyes softened, no doubt thinking I was being sweet, but I was just stating facts. I wouldn't hide how damn happy Lucas made me, and I'd take his mouth anytime I wanted.

"Okay," he said softly.

"Christ. We should get outta the car before I decide to fuck you in it."

He laughed. "Might be best. Not enough room in here really."

I snorted. "I'd make room." We got out and met at the front of the car. I took his hand and led us to the double doors. Already the music was loud, and the voices louder to make up for it.

Lucas tried to pry his hand out of mine at the doors, but he stopped when I looked down at him, and his eyes landed on the tick in my jaw from annoyance. We had to be us in front of the brothers. I wouldn't have it any other way. It wasn't like I'd screw Lucas in front of anyone. No one got to see him naked. Shit, we were just holding hands. The sooner they dealt with their own issues, the better.

I opened the door and stepped through, bringing Lucas with me. People eyed us, a lot of the brothers greeted us, and a few looked away. So far it was good. I steered us around tables, people, and stopped at the bar.

Lucas stepped up beside me and rested his elbows on the bar. He glanced around nervously, until someone called his name. His gaze swung to Kylo on the other side of the bar, and he grinned. "Kylo. It feels like it's been ages."

"It has, but shit happens and time flies." He winked. I growled under my breath. He shot me a look and laughed. "Relax, brother. We all know he's yours after claimin' him in front of everyone in church."

Lucas's gaze spun to me, and I rolled my eyes. "He's exaggerating."

"Sure he is," Lucas mumbled. He looked back to Kylo. "Since I have you here and you can't brush me off, are you going to explain why my brother said you were thinking of applying to the Polished P and P?"

Kylo laughed. "It was just a runnin' thought he overheard me sayin' to someone. I doubt I'd ever do it." He glanced around. "Now, what can I get you two?"

"Rum and Coke, and Lucas'll have a vodka and soda."

"Got it." He grinned.

When he was out of earshot, Lucas turned to me and asked, "Do you believe that?"

I didn't. He wouldn't meet Lucas's gaze, but for a fact, I knew he hadn't actually applied as yet.

"Not really."

He hummed under his breath. "Yeah, me neither."

Leaning in, I placed my hand on his shoulder and applied a little pressure. "Might just have to wait and see. He'll probably come to you when he's made up his mind." If he didn't, I'd squish him like a bug for upsetting Lucas.

Lucas smiled up at me. "Thanks, Wade." His eyes widened. "Should I call you that here, or should I use Wreck? Oh, heck, I didn't even think to ask beforehand."

Chuckling, I shifted my hand to his waist and told him, "Relax. You can call me Wade whenever and wherever."

He nodded. "Okay. All right, that's good."

Fuck me, he was damn cute.

All I could think was how lucky I was that Lucas had moved in with Saint. It was likely I wouldn't have met him and fallen for the guy. Dipping down, I kissed his neck.

"Jesus, are we gonna have to put up with this shit all the time? My gut won't take it," Duck, who stood down the bar a bit, commented.

Lucas's hand fell over mine and gripped as anger filled me.

"Fuck off, Duck," I snarled. Who the fuck did he think he was? He was still fucking fresh at being a full member. He had no damn right speaking to me like that, and he'd soon find out.

"How about you keep that crap to your room, Wreck?"

"Why are you looking anyway if it makes you sick?" Lucas asked, surprising me. Then his cheeks heated, and I knew he probably hadn't meant to voice his question.

"What the fuck you sayin', fag boy?" Duck clipped as he straightened. Some other brothers told him to shut up, one even tried to grab his shoulder, but Duck shook him off. "I didn't join this club to see gay shit. No brother should be like that and then show it in front of others."

My hands fisted. "Mind your words, Duck," I told him in a clipped tone.

"Or what, Wreck?"

I moved. My feet ate up the floor in seconds and I got in his face and growled, "Or I'll make you shut the fuck up."

"Bullshit, you're all talk," he bit out and then shoved me back enough to punch me in the face. I allowed it so I could retaliate and fucking end him. However, before I could do anything, Lucas, *my* Lucas, moved, and he planted his fist into Duck's gut. Then in the next second, with a swift move, he was on Duck's back with his fingers dug into Duck's neck, behind his ears.

Duck yelled in pain and dropped to his knees. What in the fuck was Lucas doing?

"You don't touch him," Lucas shouted.

Duck gurgled and swung his arms around, but Lucas didn't let go.

"You never touch him or say stuff to anyone who's gay, you effing prick."

Duck's face was screwed up, and he nodded but yelled when whatever Lucas was doing hurt him.

"Just remember, I'm a dang doctor, and I know ways to hurt someone." With that threat, he pushed off Duck and stood, straightening his clothes.

Holy fucking shit. I'd stood dumbfounded with a chub while Lucas took on a brother.

Clapping started around us as Saint, Country, and Tech stepped forward.

Saint laughed. "Bro, it would have been more badass if you actually swore."

Lucas blushed as he looked around at the people staring at him. His chest rose and fell rapidly. Country moved close to Lucas and slapped a hand to his shoulder. "Welcome to the family, Lucas."

"That shit was awesome. You were all ninja-like," Tech commented.

Lucas blinked, his hands shaking as he shrugged. "I… um, didn't mean to. It just happened."

Holy shit. Shock rode him hard, no doubt at how he'd reacted. On instinct, he'd felt the need to protect me, and was now trying to understand it.

Tech was right; it'd been fucking awesome.

Beaming a smile down at him, I curled an arm around his waist as I leaned in and whispered, "You're all right."

His wide eyes looked up at me. "I didn't think…. It just happened. I didn't like him hitting you and then bam, something took over me and I reacted." His cheeks heated even more.

"It's okay. I'm damn proud of you."

His head jerked back. "You are?"

"Yeah, babe. It was hot to see you havin' my back."

Country clapped. "Let that be a fuckin' lesson to all. No one can tell another who to love. No one has the fuckin' right to say bull like that and get away with it. No one else has to hide when they're showin' their partner some lovin', and we don't expect you two to do it either." His eyes landed on us at the end.

"Damn right," Saint yelled.

Country looked down at Duck in disgust with his upper lip pulled up. "You don't fuckin' smarten up, you're out. Hear me?"

Duck, who was still on the ground, grunted and then stupidly said, "Didn't know you were a fag lover, Prez."

Stupid cunt just wouldn't learn to keep his mouth shut. Country's jaw clenched. "Torch, Death, take him out for an advanced lesson before he leaves the club," Country called.

"Prez, shit, fuck, no, I won't do it again," Duck shouted as Death and Torch came forward and dragged a still yelling Duck out.

"I didn't want this to happen," Lucas said softly.

Country stepped in front of him, gripped his chin, and lifted Lucas's gaze. When I growled under my breath, Country let his grip go, but he told Lucas, "Listen to me, kid, and listen well. My pa put this club together a very fuckin' long time ago. It's a place of peace, a place for brothers to come together and share in life, love, and family. We're a damn big family, and all families have their testin' members. But none, and I goddamn mean none, should treat another member like the way Duck treated you and Wreck. It's his own fuckin' issue." He turned to the room and said loudly, "and if anyone else has a problem seein' love in this fuckin' compound, no matter who is showin' it, they shut their motherfuckin' mouth, walk away, or deal with the rest of us comin' down hard on them." He glanced back at Lucas. "You're here to feel safe, to do whatever makes you happy, because you're goddamn family even before gettin' in with Wreck. Understand?"

Lucas nodded, cleared his throat, and then whispered, "Yes." He glanced to the doors where Duck had been dragged out. "But I don't want anyone hurt for being themselves."

Country shook his head. "If that's how he thinks normally, then he fuckin' doesn't deserve to be in this club. We're loyal and deal in respect for all members. His soul is tainted with ugliness. I don't want that shit to rub off on the club. That's not what we're about. Jesus, kid, not in this day and age. People need to grow the fuck up."

Lucas's sudden burst of laughter even startled himself. He covered his mouth. Then he removed it and said, "Some just aren't smart like you, Country."

Country chuckled. "Ain't that the truth. Now, let's fuckin' party and put the ugly behind us." He patted Lucas on the shoulder and stepped up to the bar.

My gut twisted in delight when Lucas moved into me, his shaky hands resting on my hips. Finally, I relaxed. He looked up at me and whispered, "Sorry for jumping in like that."

I shook my head. "Never apologize. I'm fuckin' damn proud of you for stickin' up for me, but also yourself."

He grinned up at me. "Thank you."

A couple of hours later, Lucas was slapping the bar as he tilted his head back and laughed from something Tech told him. I'd been standing away, talking with Death and Saint, but he wasn't far from my sight. It was good to see him having fun with some brothers. So far, Duck had been the only cunt who had started shit. The others had taken it in stride when Lucas and I had got close and shit. Hell, some even spoke to us when I had Lucas leaning against my front and an arm across his chest.

It made me feel good. Fuck, it felt like everything was as it was supposed to be in life, and usually, I wasn't someone who thought crap like that, but I did, and it was because of Lucas.

My Lucas.

Someone chuckled beside me. A swift thump in the shoulder followed, and I glared at Death. "Brother, you're not listenin' to anythin' we say. Go get your guy and take him to your room. Maybe then we can actually have a fuckin' convo."

"Jesus Christ, you know I'm cool about you bein' with my brother, but do not fuckin' talk about them in any bedroom in front of me. That's my kid brother."

I chuckled. "Who I'm gonna take to my room," I told him, smirking. He gave me the finger and stalked off while Death laughed. I quickly made my way over to Lucas, Tech, Kylo, and Torch.

They all stared at me, grinning.

"What?" I asked.

Kylo snorted. "We told him it wouldn't be long before you were over here, draggin' him away from all the looks you were givin' him."

I shrugged and held my eyes on a blushing Lucas. "They were right." Reaching out, I took his hand and led him away from the taunting group.

"Torch wouldn't say what happened to Duck. Do you know?" Lucas asked.

I did, and I wasn't sure Lucas needed to know or really wanted to know. I worried he would see us as bad people. I stopped in the hall, turning into him. I took a breath. "You know who we are, yeah?"

His head tilted to the side as he looked up at me. "What do you mean?"

"My brothers and I, we're bikers. We live different, have our own set of rules, and we'd die by them."

He swallowed. "Um… okay."

"He disrespected you, me, and the club. He needed to pay."

He nodded. "Honey," he whispered. "You can tell me anything. I know you disappeared for a while. I'm not stupid." He lifted my hand up and ran a finger over my knuckles. "You went out and saw him with Country. I just need to know if I need to prepare myself to lie to the police or not. How far did it go?"

I could see the trace of concern in his eyes, but he also had trust, and him holding onto me told me so much more than anything.

Fuck me.

Fuck, fuck me.

He was damn perfect.

I crowded him, pushing him back into the wall. "He's alive, kicked from the club, but alive."

He ran his hand up my stomach, my chest, and cupped my neck. "Okay, Wade. Now, can you show me your room… I presume we were heading there?"

"Fuck yeah, we are," I growled low, and then shifted back to pick him up over my shoulder. He let out a squeal, and I slapped his ass walking the rest of the way down the hall. He laughed until I ran my hand up the back of his thigh and gripped his ass cheek.

He gasped. I opened my door, pushed it wide, and stepped in. I planted him on his feet, kicked the door close, locking it behind me.

"Get naked for me, Lucas," I ordered and leaned against the door with my arms crossed over my chest.

He licked his lips and started with his long-sleeved top by dragging it up his body and throwing it to the floor. His shoes and socks were next, then his jeans. He slowed down on those and drew them down his legs while watching me palm my cock behind my jeans.

Christ, he could always make my dick hard in seconds. Just looking and watching everything he did, the way his hair fell in his eyes all the time, the way he smiled, smirked, teased. Even listening to him could bring a fat one.

"Bend over, hands to the bed," I clipped.

He did, and then looked over his shoulder to see me removing my vest and tee. I was too fucking eager, so I kept my jeans on but undid them as I walked to my bedside table and grabbed a condom and lube.

Moving in behind him, I dropped the items to the bed and then placed my hands on his back and ran them leisurely down over his warm, smooth skin. He shuddered under my touch, bringing a smile to my lips.

He always reacted to my hands on him. Always.

I rubbed over his ass and then tapped hard enough for him to gasp and push back on my hands.

"Wade, please," he begged. He liked taking my cock as much as I liked giving it to him.

Goddamn perfect.

"You need me, babe?'

"Yes, always."

"Good." I grabbed the lube, spread it over my fingers, and trickled some into his crack before pulling my cock free and slathering it with more lube. I ran my other hand up and gripped his shoulder while lining up my dick to his slippery, tight hole. "You need prep?" I asked thickly.

"No. Inside me, now, please."

"Fuck," I muttered, and then pressed in gently. He pushed back, but I tightened my grip.

"I'm okay, honey," he reassured me, but he was still tight, and I didn't want to hurt him. He pushed back again as he turned his head and bit down on my finger.

"Christ," I clipped, and then couldn't help it. I thrust forward, all the way in. Lucas cried out, and I stilled. "You all right?"

He panted out a breath and looked over his shoulder at me with hooded eyes and a sweet smile. "Oh yeah."

"Fuck me, you are sexy," I told him as I slowly withdrew and then pushed back in.

"Wade" was all he could say. Since his head was still turned toward me, I could see him as he closed his eyes, and when his lips parted as I hit the right spot, he begged, "Harder, please."

Jesus Christ, I wanted to sink my whole body inside him and hold him for-fucking-ever. Leaning over, I pumped my hips back and forward as I kissed his back and ran my hands over his sides, his chest, his stomach, and then I dipped one down to grip his hard cock. I slid a finger over his leaking tip and brought that finger up to lick and taste his precum.

"So good," I murmured.

Lucas hummed under his breath. He tightened around me when I curled my arms around him, one at his shoulders and chest, the other his waist, and I slowly stood him up enough while I continued to drill in and out of him. I kissed and bit at his neck. Sucked and marked.

"Wade, God, Wade. Yes." He gripped my arm around his waist and took all that I gave him, pleasuring in my assault.

"Fuck, babe, fuck. You feel so good. So damn good." I kissed his shoulder and bit there as well as I groaned when he tightened even more around me.

"Wade,' he yelled, and I knew he was coming. He pushed back on me hard and whimpered through his release. My balls drew up, my gut tensed, swirled, and shot down to my groin, and then I was coming. Groaning and grunting through it, I still moved in and out of him, and Lucas took it all.

Slowing my movements, I licked up the side of his neck and nibbled on his earlobe. "Fuckin' love you."

He sighed contently. "Love you, honey."

It was then I stilled before drawing all the way out. "Shit," I cursed. No wonder it felt fucking fantastic. "Babe, fuck, I didn't wear a condom."

Lucas yawned, stretched, and then climbed on the bed on all fours before laying on his stomach. "I thought it felt better than normal." I made a noise in the back of my throat. He glanced back. His eyes widened. "I'm negative if you're worried about that?"

I gawked at him. He was concerned I was worried about myself? This damn man. "No, babe, I knew you would be, but I hadn't told you I was negative, which I fuckin' am, but—"

"Wade." He grinned. "I trust you. You wouldn't have taken me without subconsciously knowing you weren't putting me at risk. Now get in here and cuddle me."

My body unlocked. The freak-out I'd started to have vanished since Lucas was being cool about it all, and shit, maybe he was right. Deep down, I knew I wouldn't risk anything when it came to him.

I walked to the side of the bed, planted a fist beside his head, and leaned in for a kiss. "Gotta clean you up, babe, and we're doing it again, if you're not too sore."

"Oh, I'm up for that."

"Good." I grinned, and for the damn billionth time, I couldn't help but think how right he was for me. Hell, I was already growing hard just thinking of going in ungloved.

"Where do you want this?" Dad asked as he came through the front door of our place.

I glanced up from unpacking my own box in the kitchen and smiled. "In the movie room, please."

"If I can find the room. I've said it once, but I'll say it again, this place is huge." He glanced at Tech, who was wiring some cables in and around the house. Dad hummed under his breath. "Wade's real protective, yeah?"

"You could say that." Wade had Tech working around the clock the previous day to set up the security system before we moved in. Now Tech was back again to install the cameras.

Dad grunted. "Good to know my boy will be safe."

My heart warmed.

"I'll always make sure of it, Gerry" came from the hallway into the laundry room, causing Dad to scream.

"Jesus Christ, son, you need your own alarm to announce your arrival."

Wade just chuckled, and I heard Tech's own mirth.

"Now point me again toward the movie room," Dad asked. I pointed the right way, and off he went. Then Mom appeared in the archway from the kitchen to the living room just as Wade walked toward me.

"Is Gerry in here?" She moved in and dumped another box on the kitchen island beside the one I was working on.

"The movie room, Mom."

Her eyes narrowed. "Is he working or watching a movie?"

"Working. He's taken a box there."

"Well, good. I have to say, Wade, this place is amazing, and it's so big," Mom commented, but she had a gleam in her eye, so I knew something else was coming.

"That's what she said," Zion put in when he entered the room.

"Zion," Mom scolded.

Wade just grinned, while I rolled my eyes.

"Anyway, as I was saying," Mom started.

"Mom, I'm not sure where this is going, but I'm kind of scared," I told her.

Wade, Zion, and even Tech laughed.

Mom sighed. "All I'm getting at is that this place would be good for a wedding, and then there's enough room for grandkids."

"I'm out," Wade stated and quickly strode from the room with Tech climbing down the ladder and following. Zion had backed up and edged toward the exit.

Groaning, I rubbed a hand over my face. "Mom, let's not jump to that yet or in the next year or two. Wade and I are still new. We're not rushing anything. Well, besides moving in together." I let out a laugh. "Okay?" I asked her.

She smiled. "Of course, sweetheart. I'll give it a year with the way he looks at you." She spun around and walked back out, passing my brother.

As soon as she was gone, Wade walked back in. I glared at him, and he shrugged with a smirk.

Zion sighed, placing a box on the floor. "Thank fuck, she didn't start on me. She's been tryin' to set me up with all her friends' daughters."

Wade stopped behind me with his hands on my shoulders. I leaned back into his familiar touch. "Why don't you just go out with one, and then she'll probably stop."

He lifted a brow.

"All right, maybe she wouldn't, but it would be worth a try, right?"

"Yeah, maybe one date wouldn't hurt me," Zion said, off in thought about it.

Something got tipped over, or someone broke something, then I heard, "It's okay." Kylo looked around the corner into the kitchen and at us. He grinned. "Promise I didn't break it. It was already broken."

Zion snorted, then left the room. Maybe he was going to listen and see Mom about a date. It would do him good. As far as I knew, he hadn't been with anyone in a while. Well, he hadn't brought anyone home in a month.

"Kylo, I didn't know you arrived." I smiled. He returned it and walked into the kitchen.

"Hang the fuck on, how about we get back to what he broke?"

"He said it was already broken."

"You believe him?" Wade asked, his tone gruff, as if he wanted me to say no, I didn't.

"Well, yes?"

Kylo laughed. "You don't sound convincin'."

"I'm working on my acting skills."

Wade snorted, while Kylo grinned.

"How's work going?" Over a month ago, Kylo hadn't told me he was applying for a job at the Polished Pussies and Penises. In fact, my calls and texts went unanswered, and when I tried to catch him unprepared by a visit, he managed to evade me. Then when Wade told me of the night Kylo had his first job at Polished, I crashed it before he even arrived to talk with him and let him know how upset I was about him ignoring me. He'd been worried about what I thought. After a few words, he knew I wasn't the type of friend to judge his choices. Now things were settled down, and he was back in my life, which I was grateful for. When I brought the one concern I had up with Wade, about Kylo being disrespected amongst the brothers, he told me with humor, "The brothers think he's the shit. To them, fucking is fucking, and if he's getting paid a heap for it, good on him."

West, another one who had kept his application from me, appeared beside Kylo. Once more, we were back to being close and good friends. I would never want my life without them in it.

"I can ask you the same question," I said to West. "How's work going?"

Both got far off looks, and my belly dropped. I didn't like it.

Kylo shrugged. "Same old. Anyway, I better go clean up the mess. Not that there is a mess to clean up," he quickly added when his gaze went to Wade behind me.

West laughed. "I'm good too, and I'll go help him before your man kills him."

They disappeared. I tipped my head to the side and looked up at Wade. "They're both hiding something."

He dipped, kissed my lips, and said, "I'll see what I can find out."

"You think they are as well?" I asked, turning in his arms and curling my hands to the back of his neck.

"If you have a suspicion and you're wanting to find out and help them, then I'll do what I can to help. For you." What was left unsaid was that he didn't care about Kylo or West; he just wanted me happy.

My body tingled, and my heart flared with love and appreciation.

I grinned. "Have I told you recently that I think you're the best?"

"Only this mornin'."

"Well, now, you've heard it again." I kissed his chest. "Do you know what?"

"What's that, babe?"

"I think I'll leave Kylo and West alone. If they were in trouble, they would reach out for help. That I have to believe. Maybe they have something going on in their love life that they just don't want to share yet." I winked. "I have to give them time to share it when they're ready."

"Could be a good idea."

"Then that's what I'll do." I glanced at the two doorways and then back to the love of my life. "But… I mean, if you want to secretly look into it in case something bad is happening, I won't stop you."

His head dropped back in laughter. I took the chance to kiss his neck and then suck on his skin. All laughter died. He picked me up and set my butt down on the kitchen island. His hands grabbed my behind, and he dragged me forward. I opened my legs to accommodate his hips.

He leaned in and nipped at my earlobe. "I wish to Christ no one was here so I could take you over this counter."

My breath picked up, and I ran my hands up and down his sculpted chest. "Maybe we could kick them out," I suggested.

He pulled back and looked down at me. "Usually, you're the rational one."

I shrugged, my cheeks heating when I admitted, "You get me aroused easily."

His smile was smug. "Good to know. At least when everyone is gone, we'll have this entire place to ourselves."

I moaned softly. "I can't wait to test out each room."

He shook his head. "I can't fuckin' wait to spend every damn day in the same house livin' with you."

More melting feelings touched me. I dropped my forehead to his chest and blurted, "I love you."

He chuckled. "Tell me again, but do it while you're lookin' at me, babe."

Lifting my head, I slid my hands to his waist and gripped. "I love you, Wade Williams."

"I fuckin' love you, Lucas Storey." He kissed me briefly. "For-fuckin'-ever."

"This is the cutest thing ever," Mom cooed from somewhere. "Gerry, come see how cute they are."

"Lucy, get the hell away from there. Zion said they'd be neckin'."

Wade closed his eyes. "Can it be tonight already?"

Laughing, I shook my head. "We can't kick them out when there's a lot more to do."

"Dammit." He gave me another quick peck and then whispered into my ear. "Until tonight."

"Can't wait," I replied, and then with another deeper, longer kiss, we got back to work, preparing our future.

NEXT IN THE POLISHED P & P SERIES:
KYLO'S STORY

ACKNOWLEDGMENTS

Lucas and Wreck have been on my mind forever. I didn't realize it would lead me into two other books! I wanted to thank you, the reader, for taking a chance on *Wreck Me Forever*. I hope you've fallen in love with these characters and the side ones, because not only will I be writing the Polished P & P series, of just MM reads, but I'll eventually start the Diamond MC.

Many thanks go to Becky Johnson and her team at Hot Tree Editing. To Lindsey Lawson and Amanda Berry, my main beta readers who decipher my work even before it gets to the editor. To my new beta readers: Darlene Tallman, Annissia Trevion, Miranda's Book Obsessed, Casey Hassall, Nikki Horn, Allena Haskins, and Amanda Evans.

A massive thank you to Jay at Covers by Juan. He is a superstar at what he does and has brought my characters to life for the cover. I'll always look forward to working with him.

Romantic Comedies

Making Changes

Making Sense

Fumbled Love

Trinity Love Series

Left to Chance (m/m/f novel)

Love of Liberty (m/m/f novella)

The Hidden Kingdom Trilogy

A Torn Paige

A Lost Paige

A Final Paige

CONNECT WITH LILA ROSE

Web page: https://www.lilarosebooks.com/

Facebook: http://bit.ly/2du0taO

Instagram: https://www.instagram.com/lilarose78/?hl=en